INTO THE FOREST

INTO THE FOREST

A NOVEL

AVTAR SINGH

Published by Context, an imprint of Westland Books, a division of Nasadiya Technologies Private Limited, in 2024

No. 269/2B, First Floor, 'Irai Arul', Vimalraj Street, Nethaji Nagar, Alapakkam Main Road, Maduravoyal, Chennai 600095

ISBN: 9789360455798

10 9 8 7 6 5 4 3 2 1

This is a work of fiction. Names, characters, organisations, places, events and incidents are either products of the author's imagination or used fictitiously.

Typeset by Ashutosh Jha
Printed at Parksons Graphics Pvt. Ltd

For Figo, steadfast these past seventeen years.
I wouldn't know the forest without you.

'The dead know something we don't, although they keep it to themselves.'

—Angela Carter's *Book of Fairy Tales*

CONTENTS

1

WHEN YOU THINK IT'S OVER

Nearly everyone

June 2020

'Look, Herr ...'

'Call me Avtar,' says the reporter.

'Avtar? Am I saying it right?' The policewoman is pleasant, polite, patient where she could be short. There are many demands on her in this strange time.

'Very well,' replies the reporter. He isn't lying. The policewoman's pronunciation is as carefully on point as the rest of her.

'Danke. As I was saying, Nabi's story really isn't that interesting.'

'It is to me.'

'It happened weeks ago. In spring, during the lockdown. I'm told people want to forget all about that time. Do you think they will still care?'

'I need to know the story before I make that judgement.'

'Right. So, this is what happened.'

This is how a scandal finds fuel in a time of isolation, when even good intentions can miss their mark.

Earlier that year, as spring's restrictions began to bite, in every mailbox in that hitherto quiet German town beside the forest—

Dear ladies and gentlemen,

It is with great sadness that I write this letter. It is terrible, in this day and age, that I even need to say this to all of you. Have we learnt nothing from the past?

Nabi has been accepted into our community. He works at our hospital. He is in the frontline against the sickness. He risks his own life while tending to the people who have been struck down. Our people.

I have watched as his reputation has been torn down. On the basis of what? A series of inflammatory posts on social media by a young man who may be lying himself? Who admits he hasn't seen this missing woman since she came down here from her university in Berlin?

This is a time for all of us to be aware of the forces that would divide us. This is a time of reckoning for us as a people, as a nation. We must come together to move past the challenges posed by the sickness.

We can't be torn apart by people promoting their own agendas.

This young man making the accusations looks a certain way. He sounds a certain way. His appeal is easy, it is clear.

So we must be wary of it.

This other young man, the accused: he looks a certain way as well. But what is he accused of? Being different?

I know what some of you will be saying. 'What if he is actually guilty?'

I say to you, we will deal with that eventuality then. Until then, be vigilant against these divisive forces. This is not what we are.

With kind regards.

'I would look at the windows.'

'I beg your pardon?'

'When I walked, bhai. I'd look up at the windows. Especially at night.'

'You don't have to call me bhai,' says the reporter.

'But you are older than I am,' says Nabi. 'I can't call you by your first name. I won't call you Herr Singh.'

'If it makes you happy, Nabi ...'

'It does. It is what I called my neighbour back home. He was like you. Turbaned. Bearded. Dignified, like an older brother. It is the name he preferred.'

'Okay. Tell me about the windows?'

'You must know the feeling, bhai. To be in a new place. To be walking past other people's homes. To want to see inside. Don't you know the feeling?'

'You have been here for years, Nabi.'

He, Nabi, is tired, even though weeks have passed since he was dragged so unceremoniously through the mud. He is slim, of medium height. He is neatly, even stylishly dressed. But his young face is lined, his gleaming black hair disordered, a stubble on his normally carefully shaven face.

The sun is out in their quiet, prosperous little corner of Germany. The nearest city is only fifteen minutes away by train, but it inhabits a different planet. Where the two of them sit isn't quite a suburb, but it may as well be. The cars here are expensive and the houses well-kept. The schools are uniformly excellent and the kids well-behaved. Graffiti happens on walls reserved for the purpose. People smile at each other as they pass.

Nabi sits five feet from the older man, as the law still requires, though people flout it openly now. A young couple walks by, hand in hand, immersed in each other. Nabi watches them as they pass.

'It feels like they are all talking about me. Even when they don't look at me.'

'It must be hard.'

'It is very hard.'

They sit under a row of trees that shade the edge of the pond the locals call the 'See'.

Nabi knows the other man has been looking at them. 'You know these trees, bhai? We have them at home as well. They are chestnuts.'

The other man sips his coffee.

'Aren't the flowers pretty? They came together to these trees a month ago. Just like that. There they were one morning! I picked the ones that fell and put them in a glass of water. My sister-in-law would do the same back home.'

'It is nice to come home to flowers.'

Nabi nods. 'Why do you want to know about what happened, bhai?'

The older man mentions a paper in the UK that may be interested in what happened to Nabi. Its politics are impeccable. His story will resonate there.

Nabi looks unconvinced.

'People must know our stories,' says the reporter.

'Why? What good does it do?'

Nabi's colleagues at the Krankenhaus—

'He is a good man.'

'A very good man.'

'Works hard. Always smiling.'

'He always buys the coffee. Always.'

Is the coffee good here, asks the reporter.

Nabi's colleagues all laugh.

'It comes out of a machine.'

'In a plastic glass.'

'Costs 60 cents.'

'You tell us. How good could it be?'

He sips at the plastic container one of Nabi's colleagues has handed him. The drink inside is approximately the right colour. But everything else about it is wrong.

'Nabi has worked here for almost two years.'

'He was at a restaurant before. Probably off the books. But now he's paying taxes.'

'A friend of his brought him here. I think they met at the language school.'

'Wasn't she Polish?'

'She was already a nurse. She got a job last year at a private practice.'

'Good for her.'

'Her German's excellent.'

'She reads and writes it too.'

'That's the ticket, isn't it?'

The reporter didn't know that Nabi was introduced to the hospital by a woman. The surprise shows on his face. One of the women, a matronly Bulgarian, giggles around her cigarette. The other women smile as well.

'Have you met him?'

'Have you not seen that shy smile?'

'A nice young man like that, alone in this place. Who wouldn't want to pet him, adopt him, take him everywhere?'

Nabi's erstwhile friends in the same town—

'He isn't the innocent he claims to be, Herr Singh.'

'He knew what he was doing. What possessed him to pursue a local girl?'

'Local girls are off-limits?' asks the reporter mildly.

'You know what I mean. Stay in your fucking lane, man. We're all immigrants here.'

'I mean, what the fuck? Why bring attention to ourselves? Especially with this illness screwing everyone and everything.'

'Keep your head down. Work hard. Enjoy the good life here. How hard is it?'

'Yes! He has a job, doesn't he?'

'Fucking asshole.'

This is how a scandal begins.

A young man on social media—

Friends, all those who have been following and supporting me:

Nabi has stalked us from the moment he met Mia. He has added her on all social media. He has liked her photos, commented on her posts, gone on the profiles of her friends. I know he has been on mine.

She is special to me. I may not call her my girlfriend anymore, but we are close. I am in her heart still. I know this.

And now she is gone.

She isn't on her phone. She isn't on her profiles. She has disappeared. Even I don't know where she is.

Who is this man? Why is he taking advantage of this terrible time?

Where is she, Nabi? Where is my Mia?

'That boyfriend of hers is an odd chap, Herr Singh.' The policewoman studies the reporter. She is reflective. It suits her, he thinks. She could be a professor. She has the listening habit.

'Avtar,' he reminds her reflexively.

'Entschuldigung. Such a lovely name.'

'Thank you. You were saying?'

'Mia's boyfriend. Yes, ex-. He talks about himself so earnestly. You think it is a joke, but then you realise he is serious.'

'It is his generation. They've grown up online. Their selves are mirrored on a screen. Their self-image is built in the third person.'

'That is very insightful.'

'It is very made up. I just thought of it.'

'Ha. You're an amusing man. You must be, yes, to be a writer and reporter?'

'Those who live to please must please to live.'

'Quite so. So, this amazingly self-absorbed young man, with his blonde hair and muscles, first approached us a week before she actually disappeared.'

'Really?'

'Yes. But this is common knowledge now, surely?'

'I'd like to hear it again.'

'She stopped taking his calls. Then she blocked him.'

'I thought that was invisible to the person being blocked.'

'He figured it out. It isn't that hard.'

'So he called you?'

'Getting dumped is always a crime. At least when it happens to men like him.'

'Do you often get calls when people get ghosted?'

She looks at the reporter appraisingly. 'You must realise, there is a lot of sympathy for women in her position.'

'You personally?'

'The Polizei. What I feel is irrelevant, don't you think? I'm the spokeswoman.'

'But you're still an officer. And you're still a woman.'

She smiles. 'This story is not new, you know. It has happened before. It will happen again. Surely there must be other things you'd rather write about?'

The reporter looks at her silently.

She shrugs. 'When the boyfriend first called, the reporting officer was inclined to dismiss it. His first thought was that the man was egotistical. Possibly abusive. Definitely too stupid to realise the sickness had been used as an opportunity to escape him.'

'You've heard all this before?'

She nods. 'Even so, we had to investigate. Especially now.'

'Of course. She could have been sick at home.'

'Or just unreachable. Which would be fine, normally. People are entitled to their privacy. But the degree of unreachability, at this time, has gone up by many factors. You understand?'

'Privacy has a cost.'

'Exactly. We don't want anyone falling off the grid. Not now.'

'Being on the grid protects us all?'

'I couldn't have put it better myself.'

'So you went looking for Mia?'

'A few days before she disappeared. Yes.'

'Tell me about the people you saw in the forest, Nabi,' says the reporter.

'Which ones? Mia's parents? The Bosnian and her little boys? The Indian woman?'

'Indian woman? Which one?'

'She has a dog. I think her name is Ahilya. We haven't really spoken much.'

The reporter knows of the woman. The Indian community to which they both belong is a small one in this town. He is intrigued that she walks in the forest as well. 'Have you met her man?'

'The Indian woman? Or the Bosnian?'

'Either.'

'Well. The Bosnian's man has been ... away, I suppose. The sickness, perhaps. It is always just the woman and her boys. If you saw her, bhai, you would smile. You wouldn't be able to help yourself. She is an angel.'

'Beautiful?'

'Patient and kind. Those boys are the luckiest children in the world.'

'Yes. And the Indian?'

'She has a husband and one teenaged son. Nice-looking boy. I saw them just before Christmas, I think. I remember greeting them as they walked up in the forest. They said they were going home for the holidays.'

Something stirs in the reporter's mind. 'You haven't seen them since?'

'No. Why?'

The dates don't match up. 'It doesn't strike you as strange that you haven't seen them in months?'

'The world's been closed down for at least half that time, bhai. Maybe they were stuck. I had other things on my mind.'

'If they were going to India, wouldn't she have gone with them?'

'I came to this country alone. I haven't seen my family in six years.'

'Did you ever see her with anyone else?'

'The lady who owns that Biergarten up in the forest. I think they're friends.'

'Does she know you?'

'I'm sure she's seen me. I'm always in the same place. At the same time.'

That Biergarten up in the forest—

'This is a nice place,' says the reporter.

'It is perfect for me.'

'So quiet. Do you get many animals up here?'

'Vegetarians, yes. The only meat-eaters like a beer as well. Or something stronger.'

The reporter laughs with the bartender. 'Has the Indian lady been here recently?'

'Ahilya? Is she a friend of yours?'

'Not exactly. But we know of each other. There aren't so many of us Indians in this town.'

'Between the doctors at the Krankenhaus, the software engineers, and the five different restaurants, I would have thought you had enough for a song routine.' She claps her hands above her head and twirls, looking coquettishly over her shoulder.

'You watch Hindi movies,' he asks.

'Who doesn't?'

He studies her behind her little bar. She is about his own age, which is to say almost fifty, but she wears her years lightly. Her hair, her skin, the way her light eyes startle you from the adjoining dark; it is clear she isn't completely native.

'Where are you from?'

'My father isn't European.'

'But your mother is?'

'She was born less than ten kilometres from here.'

'You're a local.'

'I speak the dialect,' she agrees. It marks her when she opens her mouth anywhere else in this country.

The reporter looks around. Her space up in the forest really is beautiful. Now that the restrictions are lifting and the weather is warm, there will soon be customers around the tables outside.

He sees a movement through a window. He steps to the glass, notes the shadows from the trees that have exploded into lush life around this little bar. What a sight its lit windows must be on a winter's night. To be walking up here, to listen to the creaks and the rustles of the enclosing dark, to feel the cold at every crease in your clothing, and then to see this place.

Had it been a deer?

There is nothing. The forest has swallowed it, whatever it was.

He turns away from the window, sips the drink she has poured him.

'Would you like something to eat?'

'Are you allowed to serve me?'

'Who will know up here?'

'Everything is closed in town.'

She shrugs.

'Don't you care about the law?'

She smiles at him and his glass, so he does as well, shaking his head at his own complicity.

'Are you even getting deliveries?' he asks.

'I'm sure I have something in the freezer,' the bartender says lightly.

No, he replies finally, regretfully. One drink is as far as he'll go on this particular road.

'Ahilya is a friend,' she murmurs. 'I value her privacy. You wouldn't be looking to invade it, would you?'

'Have you ever met her husband and son?'

'What did you find when you first went looking for Mia?' asks the reporter.

'What we expected to. She was fine, and in her parents' home. Well-fed and watered and walking the family dog. A bit lonely. But who wasn't, back then during the lockdown?'

He likes this police officer, thinks the reporter. The smiling eyes that set off the dark hair corralled into a severe bun at the back of her head are of a piece with the rest of her, indicative of how every part of her treads the line between approachability and an acknowledgement of her position. At least when she's here, in this office, at this time, wearing her uniform.

What are you like when you're at home? It is a question he has had of everyone that has crossed his path these past few months.

'You spoke with her?' he asks.

'We didn't have to. It was obvious.'

'Were you monitoring her media? Her phone?'

'We don't have to tell you that,' says the spokeswoman. 'We *can't* tell you that.'

'Okay.'

'I will tell you this, though. A man who runs up in the forest every day phoned to complain about them. Even before the ex-boyfriend started raising a fuss.'

'About Nabi and the girl?'

'Yes. This man said they were sitting too close to each other. They were *obviously* not from the same family. So ... he felt it was his duty as a citizen to complain.'

'Of course it was. What did you say?'

'The officer who took the call thanked him for his civic sense and sent a man up to take a look the next day.'

'And?'

'They were sitting the required distance apart. Just the two of them. Not touching. We knew her parents were stuck in Thailand. We know he lives alone. They were absolutely in compliance.'

'End of story?'

'As far as we were concerned.'

'What about the boyfriend's rubbish online?'

'For one thing, that started later. For another ... hate crimes, racist attacks, incitement thereof: different department. You know that.'

'A busy department.'

'Getting busier every day.'

'Still,' presses the reporter, 'you knew about the poison he was putting up?'

'Do you know how many calls we were fielding every day? Kids playing football, young lovers sneaking out to hold hands, a man who stood too close at the bakery? One old tart was still turning tricks behind the bus station, two weeks after the lockdown! How else was the poor thing going to eat? After she got sick, it took us three days to track down every single man who had been with her in the previous fortnight. You think idiots like that identify themselves of their own volition?'

'I can appreciate you were busy.'

'We still are. This isn't over.'

'No. It isn't. Tell me, did you get a chance to look into that Indian lady I was telling you about? The one with the missing family?'

'They aren't missing. They just aren't here.'

'What do you mean?'

'They could be anywhere. In India. Some third country, and they're stuck there because of the sickness. Schools are online. The companies around here have asked employees to proceed on leave, or consider sabbaticals. They're certainly not expecting them to come to work. Maybe not for months.'

He nods slowly. The spokeswoman smiles at him. 'That poor woman really interests you, doesn't she?'

'Poor woman?'

'I know who she is. We know her habits. We aren't completely clueless. These last months, these new circumstances ... We know a great deal about all of you, now.'

'Didn't you always?'

'Now we can admit it,' says the policewoman lightly. 'But all that woman has had since this time began is her little dog, and that hippie bartender up in the forest.' She looks keenly at the reporter. 'She has a family, but she can't touch them. She is from a place that she can't return to, and she doesn't even speak the language of this place she's in.'

'You just described the lives of millions of people.'

'Terrible, isn't it?'

'It truly is.'

'If you ask me, hers is a far better story than poor old Nabi's.'

'The forest,' says Nabi. 'What a place it is, bhai. You know?'

'I'm not sure I do.'

'Where I grew up was small. We knew everyone. But outside, up in the mountains, the way things were then ... It was unknown. You know?'

'I think so.'

'Here, there's no such thing. I mean, things are unknown to us when first we arrive, but that is because we are strangers. We don't know the language. Everything is foreign because we don't belong.'

'You belong now?'

'I don't have to. I understand this place. I know its rhythm. It doesn't scare me anymore.'

'Okay.'

'Once you work out what the rhythm is, the rest can follow.'

'What does the forest have to do with that?'

'The forest has its own story. If you shut your eyes; if you pretend that you can't hear the cars ... while you're there, you can be free.'

'Of what?'

'All this.'

'Is all this so bad? Isn't this why you came?'

'I don't want to be free of my microwave, bhai. I love the convenience and the security. The freedom. The knowledge that when my nephew comes, he won't step on a mine. I ... all this has its own weight.'

'Sure.'

'Being so far from my family. Fitting in, getting my papers, starting their formalities.'

'Being alone?'

'Look what that bastard did to me, bhai. All this time, I kept my head down and worked hard and did everything that was expected of me. But all it took was him pointing his dirty finger in my direction, and they all believed him. Him. Not me.'

'Didn't you always know this?'

Nabi takes his time. 'Maybe I'd convinced myself otherwise. Up in the forest on my break, walking there at night. I could tell myself that I was in a place as alien to everyone else as it was to me. Especially right now, with the sickness.'

'A truly new world?'

'Not new. Just different. Where everybody was a stranger.'

'Then you wouldn't be alone?'

'I would still be alone, bhai. But so would everyone else. In the forest, we would all be the same.'

'Are you her only friend,' asks the reporter.

'Well ...' The bartender in her Biergarten considers the question. 'There's an old lady she walks with in the forest. Her name's Liesl. I really don't know what they talk about.'

'Anyone else?'

'There's another Indian woman. I forget her name. She works down at the rubbish incinerator. They don't meet that often.'

'That's it?'

'That's it. Apart from that, Ahilya doesn't have a single friend in this town.'

'Really?'

'She's been here almost a year. Don't you think that's odd?'

'The sickness is part of that, surely?'

'She would never have made her way up here if she wasn't alone.'

'She told you this?'

'She's possibly the most isolated person I know, and I live in Northern Europe. We specialise in lonely people. When I do meet her men, I'll be speaking very firmly to them.'

The thought of this curly-haired bartender ticking off a couple of Indian males makes the reporter smile.

You don't abandon a woman who is already alone,' she says.

'But the sickness—'

'I'm talking about before the sickness. When she came up here in the first place.'

'Of course.'

'The only place she really likes in this country is up here. This forest.'

The reporter considers this. His experience of Indians abroad is that the things they like are to be found in the little town at the foot of these woods. Straight roads, neat homes, traffic that follows rules. Reliable water and electricity. Shops next to each other in heated malls. It intrigues him that this forest, its solitude and sudden unexplained cacophonies, has so bewitched one of his compatriots. 'Is she from a place like this back in India?'

'City girl through and through.'

'Really?'

'She is like you. Speaks English fluently. Obviously well educated. Quite a privileged background, I think.'

'You know a lot about her.'

'She is my friend. I'm happy to introduce you. She could use another.'

'If she's so lonely, why is she hanging out in a forest?'

'You can ask her when you meet her.'

He says nothing.

'She comes around the same time every day.'

He looks away.

'Wouldn't you like to meet her?'

'You can't call someone lonely if they go looking for solitude,' he says, finally.

'Can't you?'

Up in the Krankenhaus—

'Knowing what we do now ...'

'Yes.'

'I would definitely handle it differently.'

'Not talk about it to other people.'

'No. Nor speak to the press.'

'Stay off the social media.'

'Exactly.'

'Still ... what else were we supposed to do?'

Nabi's old colleagues keep bringing the reporter coffee from the machine. He has been up to the hospital a few times now. He has drunk litres of the weak, sweet brew and he is heartily sick of it, but they bring it anyway. They want to tell him about their friend, the good man who worked with them. The man the police had come to interview, taking him into a separate room to ask him about the girl who had gone missing.

'It was a shock to all of us.'

'But to be asked is nice. You know?'

'When the news people came. Our families and friends. Everyone who knew we knew Nabi.'

'Everyone wanted a piece of him. Our piece.'

'I told you all to keep quiet.'

'Yes, uncle. You know best.'

'I told you to keep your heads down and concentrate on your work.'

'Always right, uncle. That's you.'

'If you'd just listened instead of making fun, maybe Nabi would be here, standing with us, instead of being suspended.'

'Nothing will happen to him. He has done nothing wrong.'

'They can't touch him.'

'And neither will anyone else, now! Then what happens to his family?'

The older man's colleagues look into their cups to avoid his eye, but he is incensed.

'You people. You think coming here is enough. Then you think finding a job is enough. Then your family comes and you think that's enough. That's not where it ends.'

'When does it end, uncle?'

'It never fucking ends!'

'If you don't mind my asking, Avtar ... Why do you care?'

'About whom?'

'The Indian woman's family.'

The reporter shifts in his chair. 'I don't really care. About her husband and son. But I care about her.'

'Just her?' The policewoman smiles.

'All the people left with nobody to talk to. Or touch.'

She nods. 'There are a few families up there by the forest that we keep an eye on.'

'Criminals?'

'Quite the opposite. Women with abusive husbands. Partners of gangsters. That sort of thing.'

'You wouldn't think that went on around here.'

She smiles and shakes her head. She can't tell if he is joking. 'It is hard, watching out for them all. Especially right now.'

'I can imagine.'

'Yes. More coffee?'

'I'm fine, thanks.'

'So. The morning we knew she was gone was the same day we went up to the hospital to interview Nabi.'

'When her ex-boyfriend called you in a panic because her phone was off.'

'Right. That is when we felt we had to act. Phones switched off these days is a bit of a red flag.'

'Certainly for young people.'

'Exactly. Especially now they're the only contact many people have left.'

'Yes.'

'She'd been at home the night before. The young man had been outside her house that night.'

'Nabi?'

'He called her once, from outside her home. Then once again, a few hours later.'

'His calls were answered?'

'This is strictly off the record. You understand?'

He nods.

'They spoke to each other that night. The next morning, her phone was turned off. That was the only reason we went up to speak with him. It was reasonable to assume that he was the last person to speak with her. See her.'

'*See* her? At night? With the sickness?'

She takes a moment over his obvious surprise, looks at him with an eyebrow raised. 'Haven't you spoken with her?'

'I never meant for any of this to happen to Nabi.'

'I'm sure you didn't.'

'I know what that maniac did to Nabi and his reputation.'

'Then why did you disappear?' asks the reporter.

Mia looks at him sharply. 'I didn't owe my ex-boyfriend an explanation. I certainly don't owe you one, Herr Singh.'

'Of course you don't. I'm sorry if I sound judgemental. It is ... well, it is an important question. I'm sure you appreciate that.'

'I know it is important to Nabi. He is really the only person who matters here, don't you think?'

'Then why don't you tell me?'

'Because I don't know. What can I say that will make you think better of me?'

She looks down at her coffee. The tables outside the café are crowded with the cake-and-cappuccino set enjoying their treats in the sun. The plaza beyond is filling up with people, now that the restrictions are almost gone.

She should be happy, luxuriating with the others in their freedom, returned just in time for summer. Her toenails should be painted and in sandals like the other women are wearing. But her hair looks dirty, her face is tired, and her scruffy hiking shoes look as if she hasn't taken them off since winter began.

'I don't know,' she says again. 'I mean, I know why. I'd just shaken off my old ... boyfriend. Then he started stalking me online and calling me all the time and leaving me messages. The last message was so vile ...'

'You had met Nabi.'

She nods slowly. 'That last night, I messaged Nabi to come. He could stand outside. Is that wrong?'

'Not at all.'

'People need other people, Herr Singh. This sickness, my parents not being here, that asshole in Berlin ... it all just exploded.'

'And Nabi is a good man?'

'He is a very good man. We had just made a connection. You know?'

'I know.'

'I wanted to see him outside my window. Standing on the sidewalk. I know how it sounds. How selfish. But I just needed to know that there was another living person on the planet who would come when I called and want to talk to me. I don't think I'm alone in that.'

'You're not.'

'I wanted to see him somewhere outside of the forest. I wanted him outside my house.'

'Then why did you call him in?'

'He isn't the innocent you think he is.'

'Did he make you feel unsafe?'

'Of course not. He is a kind, gentle man.'

'Then what do you mean?'

'He knew why I'd called. He wanted the same thing. I didn't take advantage of him. You must know that.'

The reporter is quiet.

'Do you know that? Herr Singh, you must understand. We *both* wanted it.'

'And after?'

'You've never wanted to run after you slept with someone? You've never wanted to be alone?'

The sun is bright behind her, a halo to match that of the dirty brown hair around her young head. She could so easily be an angel.

'The restriction on driving had lifted. My parents have a cabin in the hills. I turned my phone off and left it with my aunt. I put the dog in the car and left. I was gone for forty-eight fucking hours. How did I know what would happen? What that maniac would create with just his phone?'

'Your aunt didn't notice the fuss?'

'She is eighty. She's not on social media. By the time she figured out what was going on, I was practically home anyway.'

A thought strikes the reporter. 'Your aunt ... Is her name Liesl?'

The young woman nods distractedly. It is of little consequence to her. Her mind is on other things.

'The sickness,' she continues. 'A condom doesn't protect you against this virus. I knew Nabi was careful, and I wasn't meeting anybody. But still ... I mean, he worked at the Krankenhaus.'

'You were concerned about that?'

'I was freaking out about it, a little, yes. I don't think that's abnormal.'

'Is there anything you'd do differently?'

'I'm not sorry we were intimate. He is allowed that. So am I.'

He shrugs. 'There is something that concerns me, though.'

'What?'

'Aside from the police and your parents, a few people who are respecting your privacy, such as myself, nobody knows that he was in your house, at your invitation. Why didn't you say it openly once you knew what was going on? Don't you think it would have helped?'

'I wanted to. Nabi said no.'

'Why? Why did he say no?'

'The restrictions, maybe. If people found out we had been together … Perhaps his immigration process would suffer? I don't know. He won't talk to me anymore. I've reached out to him so many times. I've told him I'll do anything. Go online, record a video, talk to the papers, tell them whatever he wants me to say. He won't speak to me.'

'Does that hurt?'

'What hurts is not having somebody to sit next to in the forest. Not having tea in the morning with a man who listens. Not having a friend.'

He wants to lean across and pat her on the shoulder, to tell her it will be alright. He doesn't, because it isn't appropriate. And it isn't true.

'When did your parents return?'

'Yesterday.'

'What are your plans?'

'I go back to Berlin this weekend. My university may open again.'

'Are you ready?'

'My friends will protect me.'

He raises an eyebrow. Mia shrugs and smiles. 'I'll have to deal with that asshole sooner or later. I'm a big girl. I'll manage.'

'Right.'

'Herr Singh?'

'Yes?'

'Will you tell Nabi he doesn't have to answer my calls? Just tell him, my dog and I miss him, and we're still on the bench every morning. I have my mug with me, if he wants to come up to the forest again.'

'Why didn't you tell me, Nabi?'

The young man looks at the reporter obliquely. 'What good would it have done?'

'Are you protecting her?'

Nabi shrugs. 'It might have helped me then, to have said something. But how would it help now?'

'Are you shielding someone else?'

'I work in health. It is a time of sickness. We shield each other.'

The reporter sighs. The other man's levity is ill-judged, in his opinion. But he isn't the police. Nobody *has* to tell him anything.

'The Krankenhaus knows I was with her,' continues Nabi.

'How do they know?'

'The police told them. Public safety.'

'Is that why you're suspended?'

'Partly. Though the restrictions were on the verge of relaxing at that time anyway, so that's in my favour. They've monitored my activity, the people I've met. They know I'm not sick. I'm not a threat to the community.'

'But your behaviour with her showed bad judgement.'

'Yes. It really did.'

'Do you think they'll use it against you?'

'My supervisor is a good person. She understands how hard all this has been.'

'Mia's ... "disappearance"?'

'The sickness, bhai. The harder you have to monitor people's behaviour, the gentler you have to be when they mess up.'

'Your superiors are gentle?'

'They take care of the sick. They have to be.'

'I wish I shared your idealism.'

'I neither smoke nor drink. How else can I deal with this situation?'

'I wish you drank, Nabi. I've had my fill of coffee.'

The younger man laughs. It is a lovely sound. His eyes aren't tired anymore when he is happy.

'Why don't you see Mia again?'

'What good will it do?'

'She wants to be your friend.'

'She will return to Berlin. She will meet someone else. Get back with that man who ruined me.'

'She won't do that.'

'Why wouldn't she? Why shouldn't she? She owes me nothing.'

These past days and weeks, as they've drunk coffee and watched people take off their masks as the restrictions eased, this hasn't changed. The young man's insistence that the woman he wooed with tea owes him nothing.

The reporter finds it endearing and infuriating at the same time. 'This will pass, Nabi.'

'How do you know that?'

He doesn't, of course. Nobody does. 'How long will the enquiry at the hospital take?'

The young man waves his hands. He doesn't know. But he isn't too worried. 'As long as nobody else comes forward and says that I was with her physically, my supervisor tells me my job is safe.'

'You want to go back to the hospital?'

'It is what I know. I need a good job. My family can't come across otherwise.'

'Do they still want to come?'

Nabi shrugs. But his eyes are tired again. He doesn't know, anymore. 'I have to believe they still want to come. Why did I make this journey in the first place if they don't?'

'That's what families do, Nabi. You are the younger brother. The future. Perhaps getting you out was enough.'

He looks away. 'Not that, bhai. Don't put that on me.'

'Do you want them here?'

'There are two ways to have families in these places for people like us. Bring your old family across. Or make a new one here.'

'You can't have both?'

'I'd like to think that's possible.'

'It is.' The reporter reaches across to put a hand on the young man's shoulder. It is the first time he has actually touched him. 'It is, Nabi.'

The Afghan looks at the older man with his warm, tired eyes.

'She called me to her window, bhai. She invited me in.'

'Was it everything you expected?'

'It should have been.'

A gaggle of geese walks across the pavement in front of them, bound for the lake. A child, no older than three, runs up to them till one of the older geese hisses at her. Her mother drags the child away, protesting.

The geese, full of grace again, float away on the placid water. The young mother leads her now-crying child away to placate her at the ice-cream kiosk. Little flocks of people, their masks hanging around their necks, cluster around the vendor.

'It is my nephew's birthday today.'

'Sweet boy?'

'The best.'

'How old is he?'

'Six.'

Nabi will speak to the boy he loves with all his heart in the evening. Before that child he has never met sleeps.

'None of this is Mia's fault,' says Nabi quietly.

'Then why won't you see her?'

Nabi shrugs. 'It was always just me,' he whispers. It is almost inaudible to the other man.

'I'm sorry?'

'I'm not sure she was ever really there, bhai.'

'Where?'

'Outside *my* window. Looking at the light inside.'

'I don't think I'll be bothering you again.'

'You are always welcome. Our doors are open to any citizen of this town. I've enjoyed our conversations these past weeks.'

'Thank you for everything. The insight. The information. The coffee.'

'You like our coffee?'

'Best I've had so far.'

The police spokeswoman acknowledges the compliment. She knows it is well deserved. 'I hope we were helpful?'

'Very.'

'Will you be writing it for a newspaper?'

'I'm not sure there is a story here. And it was a while ago.'

'It is your decision to make. You do remember I told you Nabi's tale wasn't worth retelling?'

She *has* told him, time and again.

'You understand, what we discussed off the record must remain so.'

'Of course.'

'Perhaps you will find other things to write about. Such strange things have been happening these past few months.'

The reporter can only agree. 'He isn't a bad man, you know.'

'Nabi? Oh, we know that,' she says lightly.

He looks at her, a question in his eyes, but she just smiles and rises to her feet.

She walks him to the door, past the reception area, where people are beginning to queue again. He keeps his distance from the line of waiting citizens, waves his hands under the disinfectant dispenser set up at the door. His mask is already on.

'They worry you?'

'It is odd,' he admits. He has gotten out of the habit of other people.

'There is one positive about these restrictions lifting,' she says reflectively.

'Just one?'

'From the police perspective. Now that people aren't locked down, we will know when something is wrong. God only knows what horrible things have been happening inside people's homes. Within their locked-down lives.'

He looks at her. People report the horrible things that happen to them, surely. But everything he has seen in his life tells him that isn't true.

We have our lives with other people. Even during a plague. The web that ties us to each other isn't so easy to cut oneself free of, and the wounds we carry from those closest to us remain hidden even in the light of day.

The masked strangers, only their eyes visible, five feet distant from one another; they ignore him and the policewoman as they walk past.

Be well, she says. Be safe. Now that things are opening up; now that people think the worst is behind them. This is when we have to be most alert.

She waves as he walks away.

He knows where he has to go.

Away from the well-ordered town, up the hill, into the forest.

She looks almost feral.

She is no longer the person the reporter saw almost a year earlier at a reception for recent arrivals organised by the local Indian community. She had been immaculate; nails painted, hair coiffed, sari worn just so. Her eyes shone.

Her family were at her side.

There had been no illness and no isolation.

Today her hair is frizzy from the forest. Her hands look uncared for. There is no make-up on her face.

Her eyes are still bright, though. Her dog, off the leash, ambles over. She sniffs at his leg.

'You smell my dog,' he murmurs. He bends to make friends.

'You have one too?'

'Well. He's not much of a dog, really. He's never been a genius. Now he's slow and old as well.'

'But he is yours.'

Yes, thinks the reporter. He is mine.

'I believe you've been looking for me,' says the wild-haired woman.

The bartender watches the two Indians from her perch behind the little bar.

'You're Ahilya.'

The wild-haired woman says nothing. It wasn't a question.

'I'm—'

'I know who you are,' she says. 'Are you always in your stories?'

'I don't have to be in this one.'

She nods slowly, then looks away. 'I may leave.'

'Where would you go?'

She shrugs.

'Why?'

'Now that I can leave, why would I stay?'

'Your family ...'

'This isn't about them either.'

No. He sees that now.

'Such a strange time.'

'Utterly mad.'

'I have kept a diary since I came,' she says.

To maintain a record is only fitting. It will help to have things written down, when those to come question the remembrance of it. When it is time to bear witness that all of this actually happened.

He wants to know, he says. The events of that spring—

Just a few weeks ago, she murmurs. But it feels as if an age has passed. 'Can you keep a secret?'

He has no answer to such a question.

She smiles. Her face is transformed. 'Perhaps I'll show you my diary. Introduce you to a few people before I leave. Would you like that?'

She whistles, her dog trotting to her side. 'Walk with us?'

They pass together, into the forest.

2

INDIFFERENCE

Ahilya

2019

July xx

They're still asleep.

He's snoring even though he's on his side. How can a man make a noise like that and live?

Our son is in his own room. Two days off the plane, and already his room smells like feet.

I'd go mad if I didn't have my dog. She gets me out of the house. This place my husband found for us before we even got off the plane in this new country.

It is still so early. The sun rises behind the little hill our house sits under, the hill I climb with my dog. I can see the sky lightening over the small town we have moved to.

Where my husband now works. And my son will go to school.

It isn't even 5 a.m., and the sky is already pink.

This place is completely mad.

At least I have my dog.

Aug x

We're starting to settle.

Our son still sleeps all the time. He says he's jet-lagged. But I see his computer's light on under his door at night. If he won't fall asleep, how will he wake up?

My husband has started at work. He likes the people at his office, he says. They speak English. When he wants to speak his own language, there are plenty of Indians in the larger office he can speak to.

The other Indians in his company are mostly South Indian.

Well, of course they are.

You'll meet their wives soon, he said last night. We were sharing a glass of wine. Like we used to at home.

Yay.

They may be nice women, he said. He was defensive.

Vegetarians with caste marks on their foreheads and right-wing politics? I can't wait.

At least I have my dog.

Aug x

She loves the hill behind the house. It is covered with trees. What are these trees? They stand close together and their leaves are dense, and when we walk under them, the sky is obscured.

I like the noise the wind makes in them.

She pulls at her leash. I was warned it is illegal in this country to let her off, but I've seen other people allowing their dogs to run into the forest to do their business. But we are new here. I don't speak the language. I worry about breaking the rules.

There are so many rules.

I'm still getting used to picking up her shit.

Not that picking up her poop in a plastic bag is guilt-free.

Europe is just going to have to make up its mind which is worse. Dog shit or plastic. Either way, it can let me know.

You can bury her poop, my son said.

Why don't you come with me and demonstrate?

He disappeared back into his room.

She is his dog too. She isn't in our home just for the cuddles. When she's sick; when she grows old; when she shits ...

Still, I like walking her up the hill, into the forest.

It is a quiet place. Green and soft.

Welcoming. For both of us.

Aug xx

At least the shops have beef.

Walking into a butcher's shop is like entering a fairyland. This is something I've looked forward to. To have good meat, to be able to cook it at home, to eat it whenever I want. I can eat pork without worrying about tapeworm. The vegetables in the market have so much flavour.

I know this because I'm cooking all the time.

He promised he'd help with the house. We knew we wouldn't have servants, anymore. But he is so busy, he says. His job is so new, and he is working so hard to make an impression. He is too tired when he comes home.

Let the mid-year review pass, he says. Things will be different.

Besides, there is always our son.

He cornered our son over dinner last night. You have to help your mother, he said.

You see, he said later. I've told him. You'll have help now.

Then why am I mopping their pee off the toilet seat every day?

I should tell them they have to sit down and do their business from now on. If necessary, I'll show them how.

She pooped by the path this morning. I looked around, then kicked some mud and a broken branch over it.

Good girl, I whispered in her ear.

Aug xx

It is so warm here still.

He had to go out and buy fans last night. He muttered about the cost, said we could sleep without sheets. What is the point of buying something you'll only use for two weeks in a year, he complained.

We slept better with them. I liked the sound they made. It was familiar.

It is so quiet here.

Too quiet.

No vendors in the morning. No traffic noise. No horns.

No people.

His mother is still in Delhi. My family is in Mumbai. Our cook and maid and driver are now with other people. Other families will complain of the noise they make when they talk to each other on the landings of those distant places.

But the fan sounds like home.

Two weeks of hot weather. Then the fans won't be required.

In three weeks, my son will be at school.

What will I listen to then?

Aug xx

We went swimming yesterday. The public swimming pools are beautiful. Slides for the kids, diving boards, lawns around the pools for people to sunbathe, even a restaurant to get lunch.

A little bit of heaven.

I was worried I'd be surrounded by thin girls in bikinis. But even the fat grandmothers were wearing two pieces. They looked, I realised, like me.

Then I wasn't so happy anymore.

I noticed he was looking around with bright interest. It would have made me angry back home. Here, it just made me giggle. A thin-legged Indian man, hairy paunch dangling over tight swimming trunks, ogling women who didn't know he was alive.

My son, though. I threw him a towel to drape over his middle. There's no need to advertise your adolescence.

I mean, really.

Aug xx

We had sex last night.

I can't remember the last time. It was certainly the first on this continent.

Was it because of the women by the pool yesterday? Was he thinking of them, one of them, all of them, while he pawed at me?

I haven't pictured his face for years. Whatever gets him in the mood is fine by me.

But he was so smug after. As if he'd done me a favour.

What did he want? A high five? A sandwich?

His smugness made me angry. I told him as much.

He grumbled he couldn't remember the last time I said I enjoyed sex.

Well, how would he? He wasn't there.

Aug xx

This place can be so beautiful.

We went together, as a family, to an old convent nearby. It was like something out of a book. Old turrets, ruined walls, secret passages. But it is completely real.

The kitchen had huge iron ranges that burnt wood and coal. How large were the pots the nuns put on the flames? How did they get them up there?

What made them come here, to be free of the world of men, to kneel and wash and cook and pray?

It was a calling, explained the guide. Of course, it was also a way for women to be guaranteed food and protection. At that time ...

We all nodded. At least, the women did. He and my son were looking for cellular coverage.

The faces of dead saints glared down on the space between the two huge fireplaces in the winter dining room. A small price to pay, those hideous old men leering down at you, if you were safe and warm.

In the summer dining room, the light streamed through the old glass windows and the polished floor shone. The tables were pushed to one side, but I could imagine them arranged to make the most of the warmth, generations of women laughing as they bustled about, the glow of late afternoon softening their habits and setting their faces on fire. Wearing the clothes they had stitched, the food from their fields and pens flavoured with the herbs they grew.

Outside was a little graveyard, full of the memorials of local notables. One old woman had made it to a century. I wondered how many of the people with the same last name had been her children and grandchildren. How many times had she been present at their gravesides?

When her time finally came, was it a relief not being in the audience anymore?

The old convent's turrets and windows were gleaming in the afternoon sun as we drove away.

Aug xx

So warm, still.

I've hung bird feeders in the old tree outside our front door, put water out in little plastic tubs. Not that the local birds need it. There is water literally everywhere.

But leaving water out for them ... That too is a reminder of home.

We had dinner last night at a beer garden just up the hill. It is run by friendly immigrants who welcomed our dog. They know me from my walks with her.

Last night was a surprise for the boys. Something I could introduce them to.

It was so nice to sit outside and chat in the sunlight. She sat at our feet and played with the other dogs, and our son actually took her for a walk down the road while he and I finished our beers.

Come here a lot, he asked me.

Now and then.

So that's where the housekeeping money is going.

I wanted to stab him in the eye.

I'm just saying, he mumbled at me.

Fuck you.

What? What did I say?

You're an asshole. Just saying.

Aug xx

Our son started at school today.

My husband's at work.

My dog is at my feet.

It is so quiet.

What am I going to do all day?

Sept x

The forest behind us is really quite something.

Normally we walk for about fifteen minutes. Today, we were up there for hours.

We went to where we normally turn back. There's a little road we would have to cross, otherwise. She looked at me this morning when we reached it. As if to say, 'Why not?'

What would we be doing at home?

We crossed to the woods on the other side. The trees grew close over our heads. It was cool, but I still got sweaty.

I'll bring a little backpack with some water tomorrow. For both of us.

And proper shoes. I mean, if I'm going to hike …

Sept x

There was absolutely nobody up there. Just the two of us.

I let her off her leash completely. She didn't go far. She was unsure herself. But she ran and ran, as long as she could see me.

My son used to be like that when he was small. We would go to a park near our house in Delhi every evening when it was cool enough. He would charge about as if he'd been unleashed. He would swing and climb and run, but only as far as he could still see me.

I loved that about him, that I didn't have to watch for him. He took care of that for both of us.

My sweet, careful, loving son.

Who lives behind a locked door, now. And goes to an alien school.

I asked him about it every day this week when he came back home.

Had he made friends? Enemies?

Was the coursework easy?

What were the girls like?

Anything.

I wish he'd talk to me.

He doesn't talk to me either, said my husband. I told him I didn't find that comforting.

He's fine. He's a teenager. We know that. But what if something is wrong? How will we know?

Check his social media, he said.

Really? You think that's okay? I mean, ethically?

No, it really isn't. Leave him alone.

Listen...

Leave me alone too, please. I have to be up in six hours. Good night.

I don't put anything important on my social media. How will anyone know if something's wrong with me?

Sept xx

What are these birds in the trees?

They look like mynahs and bulbuls. But surely they can't have followed me all the way here to northern Europe?

At least they don't need visas. Or language classes.

But I'd like to know what they're called.

And these trees. I can see now that they're not all the same species. Some have smooth bark, and others are rough.

My dog ran into the undergrowth today. She was chasing something. A squirrel, I thought. Then I saw a rabbit jump across our path.

Right across us!

He was too quick for her. He disappeared into the forest. She came panting back to me.

I think both of us enjoyed that. A little bit of the wild, above our home in this new place.

Don't they eat rabbits here?

Sept xx

My son has two other Indian children in his class. A boy and a girl.

She's nice enough, according to my son. But he's unsure about the boy, who is hyper-competitive. Nothing wrong with that, said my husband. Means he'll go to a good university and get a good job.

My son rolled his eyes. I think I did too.

I hope he was joking.

There was a potluck dinner at my son's school yesterday. We took a bowl of biryani. Chicken. As far as I know, not a single religious group is currently anti-chicken. Can't be too careful, in an international school.

The other Indian couples came running over.

Oh, biryani. How lovely.

You eat meat? How interesting.

Aren't you both Hindu, though?

I mean, what do you say?

At least one other Indian couple is non-vegetarian, like us. Which is to say, she eats meat, and her children do. But she still has to provide her husband with his two vegetables and fresh rotis when he comes home.

What to do, she laughed.

What were the others like?

Techies and their wives. Here on contract. Their companies pay for the school. Everything else, they save.

You mean, for travel and things like that?

She smiled and poured us each a glass of wine. Then she patted my shoulder.

They're nice enough, really. They're kind and they're helpful. You'll see. You'll get used to it.

Two foreign women came over and cooed over my biryani.

But isn't it best enjoyed with your fingers?
Yes! I saw it on YouTube! How do you get your hands clean after, though?
Surely your fingers must smell later, with all the spices you use?

My husband was talking to one of his colleagues. My son was in a corner, standing on the edge of a small group of his classmates. He was smiling, but not saying anything. Then one of them put an arm around his shoulder and dragged him in, and I heard my son laugh across the room.

I've always loved that sound.

There was a third woman now, twittering at my shoulder.

We should add you to our coffee group. Would you like that?
Of course you would. We go to different cafes during the day.
Can't hang around school all day.
Can't start drinking while the sun is still up.
It is nice to see one of the Indian girls with a glass of wine in her hand, isn't it?
She's in the right spot.
Right by the bottles!

I smiled as they took my phone number. The other Indian woman with a glass of wine in her hand caught my eye from across the room and winked.

I wished I was in the forest with my dog.

Sept xx

I wrote to my old boss yesterday. I knew what she would say, but I felt I had to ask.

She can't use me from abroad, obviously. What she needs is a person in India. To hold the interns by the hand. To check the briefs they write. To be the big sister to our charges, and represent them when nobody else will.

She can't pay me here anyway. How would she? Our little organisation can't afford to pay international remittance fees. It's hard enough to raise the money in the first place.

If you want to stay involved, she said—

She knew my commitment to the cause. She told me to volunteer; to continue to do what I'd always done, read the cases and make the briefs. My name would still be on everything.

I was still in the fight, on the right side. I was still one of *them*.

Besides, I needed something to do. Right?

I can't believe I actually thought about saying yes. It's a good thing I was in the forest with my dog. I sent her a message after saying the signal had dropped.

Who says good people don't ask for freebies?

I told my husband when he came home.

Well, what do you expect? You've known they were broke for years.

We didn't do what we did to get rich, you know.

Good. Because if getting rich was the plan, I'd have to say you failed.

I couldn't believe him.

I mean, look at you. All that drive from when we met in law school ... Where did it all go?

What happened to you? I remember a man talking about all the pro bono work he was going to do. Do you think the world needs another corporate lawyer? Does your fucking company need another one? What are you, one of fifty?

My company pays for us to be here.

You wanted this.

If you don't, you're further gone than I thought.

I turned away.

He was sorry, he said that night. He was mumbling about how stressed he was against my back. The engineers had been fudging the technical data for years and they'd just discovered they'd been non-compliant all that time and he didn't know what they were going to do about it, and—

Shut up.

What?

Fuck you and your company.

Sept xx

It is cold.

We've been wearing jackets in the evening for a couple of weeks, but today was really, really chilly. Grey, misty, some rain as well.

A wet cold that settles in your bones.

I called him to ask whether we should turn the heat on.

It's always on. We have warm water, right?

Look, in case you've forgotten, I'm from Mumbai. Hot water comes from the bloody stove. What the hell are you talking about?

He actually sighed.

We just have to turn the radiators up.

I tried. They won't work.

Well, get someone in.

Who should I call?

He sent me the landlord's number. Who sent me a workman's number. Who speaks no English. I have no idea when he's coming.

If he's coming.

My husband has access to secretaries. His colleagues are locals. They speak the language.

Who do I have?

Why is this my job?

Sept xx

It is autumn, apparently. The leaves will soon be changing colour. And then they'll fall.

It is so different from India, where the leaves fall after winter, then come back in their new colours.

The first leaves are already beginning to appear on the paths we walk. There's a bit more light on the forest floor. I'm beginning to see things I didn't earlier.

There are painted lines on some of the trees. Red, green, occasionally white. What do they mean?

Are these trees marked for cutting down? Are they dead? Sick?

Is this some woodsman's code? Or a student's joke?

We share the forest with a little family. A young woman and her two children. She carries the smaller one still, while the other one runs and runs.

The mother has quiet eyes, but these past few days, now that she recognises me, she smiles.

I see them every day.

My dog knows them too, and she goes across to say hello. The children make such a fuss over her.

She dragged me into a small clearing today, after the family passed. She wanted me to follow.

There, in the clearing, was the bust of a man. It sat on a tree stump. It was cut out of wood.

I sat down on a dead tree while I waited for my dog to return. I heard a small bird scratching among the roots close to me, but I couldn't see it. There were insects about my head and I could smell the damp earth.

The man was to my side. There were deep scores in his forehead and there was a bit of metal jammed into his wooden temple.

He was screaming.

Oct x

It is definitely autumn. I felt vaguely guilty about having the heat on earlier. Now, we need it.

The rain is freezing cold. Everywhere we look, people are wearing scarves and hats. Soon they'll be wearing gloves.

We need hats and gloves. He can't say the cold will only last two weeks. Even he knows better than that.

Oct x

Our things arrived today.

I didn't believe it would matter so much to me.

But it does.

To have these things again. These photos. These carpets.

These memories. It is like my house is full of friends again.

Just like home, he said. See?

No, I don't see. But it is nice to have my friends back.

At least it will give me something to do. Putting everything away in the kitchen, the bathroom cabinets, the bookshelves we've bought here.

Up on the walls.

There's no need to rush.

I've got all the time in the world.

Oct xx

The movers broke the glass in one frame. I can't leave it as it is. It's a watercolour.

I need a framer who will understand what I want, and be affordable. Where do I find a framer in this place?

Oct xx

I stopped for a coffee in a little bar up in the forest. It is in an old hunter's cabin, up by itself on top of a hill.

I've met the woman who runs it. She's lovely.

She speaks English.

Her father is Cuban. He had come across for university as a young man.

It was a different world, she laughed. We were smoking together in the sun. It was warm that day.

Fidel was still a hero, it was that long ago. And her father was a handsome man. It was no surprise her mother fell in love with him.

Did she see her father often?

Not really. I visit once every few years. We talk on the phone a lot.

He doesn't want to move back here?

Too cold.

Not today.

I asked her whether there were still any wild animals in the woods.

Lots of deer. Rodents. A few pigs. That sort of thing.
No predators?
Not on four legs.

I've seen the hunters' towers by the sides of the fields. The local farmers are permitted to kill a certain amount of deer and boar. They need to be culled anyway, with no natural predators to hunt them.

A stand in our local farmer's market sells cured venison and boar sausage every weekend. It is delicious.

Were there ever bears or wolves?
Centuries ago. Now the only wolves around here drive station wagons.

My dog snoozed at her feet in the sun.

Have a drink next time. I run a bar, you know.
Done. I'll help you stay in business.

Her laughter followed us down the hill.

We passed the little family again, the calm quiet mother, her wide-eyed children. They knelt to say hello to my dog. They speak more to my dog than they do to me.

The forest is in flame.

It is red, it is ochre, it is orange, the whole of it shot through with green. The leaves fall around me like snow.

There are more and more leaves on the ground. They don't crunch underfoot. It is too wet for that.

How would a little animal know that a hunter was on its track?

My dog pulled me off the path. I wanted to go home, but she was insistent.

A dead rabbit lay under a tree.

Its neck had been torn open. I could have stooped to feel it, see if it was still warm. I could have waited to see whether whatever had killed it would come out of the shadows.

Come on, girl, I whispered to her. Let's go.

Oct xx

He went home to India today.

Work trip, he said. But his work is here, surely, protecting his shitty company from the consequences of its shitty malpractices.

His mother will make a fuss over him. Give him whatever he wants to eat.

One week of having his tea brought to him on a tray.

What would you like me to bring back, he asked.

He had my list.

That's all kitchen stuff. What about something for you?
I'd like to come home with you.
Not this again, please.
Fine. Will you bring back some barfi?
Of course I will. Anything else?
That's all.
Can you stop resenting me? Please?

Sure. I'll get right to it.

I'll be drinking wine and watching TV once my son's asleep.

It is good to know that nothing will change while he's away.

Oct xx

Our first Diwali when we're not at home.

The local Indian group invited me to a dinner. I should have gone, really.

But to go alone, without my husband; to have to put up with that …

I had my son help me put up some lights. Then we went to a local Indian restaurant. My god, that boy can eat. He's become a man.

He was in such a good mood. Perhaps he was trying to make up for his father's absence. Perhaps he just enjoyed having me to himself. He let me hold his hand and he talked and talked, and I just looked at him and listened and spoke only when I had to.

The owner came up later.

Good-looking boy, he said. He'd been watching us chatting with each other. He wished his son talked to him like that.

I was so proud.

Poor man, he had no idea I talk mostly to myself.

Nov x

We saw deer in the forest today!

Not just one. A family. The first one I'd seen saw me looking at it. It turned and walked away, then a little group emerged from behind the trees and walked up the hill as well.

Are there no hunters in these woods? Or do the two of us just look harmless?

I tried following them, but they were too quick. They barely seemed to be moving, but they melted away in seconds.

I only saw them because the forest is thinning.

I see things now I had no idea about. There are houses on the other side of the hill. This is the first time I've seen them.

My god, when all these trees are completely bare—

What will this forest look like then?

Nov x

How can he watch these things?

On our family computer. Has he no shame?

Oh god. Was it our son?

Don't they know I use it too?

Don't they care?

Am I invisible, now, to both of them?

Who do I bring this up to?

Nov xx

Look, it wasn't me.

Then it was him.

Yes. He's that age.

It is still revolting.

Umm.

Is this what he thinks sex is?

It is everywhere, you know.

That makes it okay?

That makes it available.

Will you talk to him about this?

I really don't ...

Will you fucking talk to him?

Nov xx

I'm not sure it was our son.

He was so reluctant to talk to our boy. It was probably him.

Not that he's wrong. This rubbish is everywhere.

This is what my son will grow up thinking is normal.

A woman in the forest, in front of a group of masked men.

She may have wanted it herself, he said. *I* was the last person he would have expected to be so judgemental. So middle class.

I didn't care about *her* and her motivations. What mattered was that two men in my house had their dicks in their hands while they watched her do it.

I'm not judging her, I wanted to scream.

I'm judging you.

Our son was at a late football practice. He was still out somewhere, doing god knows what.

My dog and I walked out into the forest. The moon was almost full. Its light streamed through the emptying trees.

It was so quiet. So bright. So cold.

I pulled my scarf tightly around my neck. She scampered in front of me, nosing this way and that.

I turned to look down the path, towards our house. Behind it was the little town we live in, its lights bright through the thinning forest.

There was nobody else at all.

I could have knelt in front of a man I didn't know. I could have done anything at all, and nobody would see.

Nobody.

Nov xx

It is frosty every morning.

Not a light dusting. Actual frost. Ice stuck to the trees, the cars, the houses. We have to scrape it off our car in the morning, our neighbours outside their homes as well, a line of people standing in the dark, working away at frozen glass.

I walked into the forest after they had left. Our steps crunched. Her hackles rose as we came up the path.

What, girl? What is it, I asked.

She stopped completely, and then she whined. She pulled at her leash, wanting to go home.

Then I saw it too.

A grey shape through the trees, at the top of the hill. I could barely make it out. The sun wasn't up, yet.

She whined and whined.

Then it was gone.

Nov xx

He had friends over from work. A man and his wife.

Someone in our house, finally. What reason is there for us to have furniture in our living room, if we have nobody to sit on it?

They spoke perfect English. They have lived in other countries. They were charming.

It is lovely to spend time with you.

It really is. And all this food!

We love Indian food. It can't be spicy enough for us.

Well, good. We were worried whether you'd enjoy it.

Oh, it's lovely. We're used to foreigners here, anyway.

Yes, you've had lots of immigration recently.

Well, when you say immigration ... These are refugees, aren't they? We'd much rather have people like yourselves, really.

Of course.

Who add something, you know? Not just take.

This is a rich country, surely?

True, but how much can we spare?

And it needs to remain our country, don't you think? Recognisably so?

We don't look like you.

Darling, please. More wine?

Later, in bed—

Such lovely people.

Fascists with language skills.

Look, it is their country. Their schools. Their children whose futures are threatened.

Then why are we here?

Nov xx

How many more leaves can these trees shed? They lie upon the paths we walk, the orange, the red and russet and deep, deep brown. They carpet this world.

These trees really should be bare by now.

The carved man is gone. Now there's the mask of a wolf, cut out of wood. It sits on its pedestal and waits for me.

There is a woodpecker in this clearing. I can hear his tapping like a hammer in my head. I've been looking for him.

No matter. In a few days, the tops of the trees will be bare enough.

Then where will he hide?

It is down to him and the ravens, now. I don't see the other birds much, anymore.

These ravens, in this empty forest in winter. Is there a more desolate sound in the world?

Nov xx

I saw the grey shape again today.

I see it every day, now. My dog has stopped whining at it. I don't think she considers it a threat, anymore.

I told him about it.

A wolf? Here?

I'm not sure that's what it is.

What would a lone male be doing down here? How would he get here in the first place?

Why would it be a male?

It's alone, isn't it?

So?

That's what males do. Females don't wander by themselves. They seek out family groups. That's basic biology.

Not just a lawyer, ladies and gentlemen. He's a Punjabi Attenborough.

There's no need for sarcasm. Anyway, as long as he stays up at the top of the forest, it doesn't really matter, does it?

No. It doesn't.

The Christmas markets start tomorrow, said my Cuban friend.

I asked her if they were nice. I've read so much about them.

They're lovely, she replied. Food. Mulled wine. Nice things and smiling people. Something to forget the months of crappy weather still to come.

She had a fire going. The three of us sat by it as the freezing rain beat down outside.

I wanted to ask her something. I felt she might have an answer.

Why do people think of the forest as male?

The people around here certainly do. Their word for it is male. In every case.

It makes me so angry.

Why?

Well, does a forest ever enter you? You enter the forest.

That is to look at it sexually.

Is there another way?

She smiled.

I asked her if she knew the works of Angela Carter. She shook her head. I told her about the beautiful stories she wrote about forests, and the things that live in them. She said she'd look them up.

I asked her to tell me what she thought if she ever found her way to them.

Why?

I told her how young I was when first I read them. A different person, living a different life.

Do you miss it, she asked. Do you miss her?

Dec x

The Christmas markets are very nice.

We've gone to a few. We walked to the nearest one, drove to the big one in the city.

My son's school has events at the local market.

His choir sang today.

He was at the back. I couldn't really tell his voice from everyone else's. But he looked so handsome.

I wanted him to walk around with me afterwards. I wanted to buy him things, to show him off, to introduce him as my son.

But I have nobody to introduce him to.

He won't introduce me to his friends. Not unless I physically walk up to them.

My husband was with us. But he met two colleagues from work and they disappeared into a tent. I saw them later, cigarettes in their mouths, glasses in their hands. They were laughing.

It started to snow. This time, I think it will stick.

This time, my dog and I will leave our marks when we walk into the forest.

Who else will have marked the snow?

I can't wait to see.

Dec x

We are to go home for the New Year.

He announced it proudly over dinner last night.

I made the arrangements last month. I didn't say anything because I wanted it to be a surprise!

I wish you'd told me, dad. I've made plans for the New Year.

What?'

I was going to go skiing. A couple of the boys were going to teach me.

Well, winter isn't going anywhere.

Neither is India.

Seriously? Do you know how much the tickets cost?

You should have told me. Just saying.

Ungrateful little shit, he said later.

He's not wrong, you know. You should have told him. He has settled, finally.

India's still home, isn't it? His grandparents are still there, aren't they?

You should have told me.

What is wrong with you people? Did you make some friends finally, without telling me? Have you got plans too? I thought you were dying to go home.

No, you're right. Of course I am. Thank you.

Dec xx

It is so cold.

The woman with the young children was ahead of us. She smiled as we walked past, one child in her arms, the other at her side. The two children gazed at us quietly with their wide-open eyes. I heard their footsteps crackling as they walked into the forest.

We continued up the path to the Cuban's bar. Christmas isn't far now. It is okay to have a drink in the afternoon.

Nobody should have to be alone.

By her fire—

That was a wolf, wasn't it?

The forest is free to everyone. You're allowed to see what you want in it.

That is cold comfort.

Make a friend of the cold. It isn't going anywhere.

A story I read ... I was still a young girl. A boy in the forest sees a girl. He knows she is human, but she is feral. She is naked. He sees her vulva.

So?

She is a wolf as well.

Far-fetched.

Fairy tales always are.

I'll tell you one, then. These woods are full of spirits.

Sprites?

Spirits. They live in the trees, in the streams, below the rocks. The forest itself is alive.

How do you know this?

I smell things.

The door swung open. The Cuban walked in.

Welcome, she said. Been here long?

Dec xx

So cold.

The frost is alive, now. It sits until the sun comes to melt it, and even then it fights.

It is on the trees, on every branch, on every bare stalk. Little spires of ice, frost blossoms that look, when the light is right, like ferns.

The trees are spectral against the grey sky. White spiders chained to the forest floor. Where would they walk to, if they were freed?

The few evergreens that dot the forest stretch their whitened canopies towards the fugitive light. The undead sentinels of winter wait quietly around them.

How will I tell anyone about this, about crunching through a white forest that has no snow? We're walking on ice, her and I. Ice, and the material remains of whatever lies on these paths. Wings. Bones. Leaves. Frozen, crackling, rendered unto dust as we pass over them.

She noses through the few dead bushes still left in the forest. I stand by the side of the path, her leash slung around my shoulders.

This is the way of the forest. Fire, frost. It has to die, in a sense.
Otherwise?
How else would it be reborn?
Is this the way of all things?

Even the ravens and that mad woodpecker are quiet.

Well? Is it?

Dec xx

The longest night of the year.

We are to leave tomorrow for India.

His company is worried. It is tracking a new illness in China. It has not been widely reported, but it is linked to a raft of absences at its plant in a city called Wuhan.

It could spread.
China is a world away.
It is an infection. It can spread everywhere.
Even so, how does that affect us?
If we don't go now, we may not be able to go at all next year.
Surely it can't be that bad?

Not a lot worried his Chinese colleagues, he said. They had known famines and revolutions. They had known hunger. But they had never seen anything like this before.

I found it hard to credit. And his company doesn't exactly inspire trust. I told him so.

We had such a fight last night.

I felt so bad for him after.

Was that love I felt at the end, as he sought to make it better? As he reached for me in desperation?

I don't know how to make you happy. I really don't.
I know.

I mean, it's my job. I'm your husband.

Please ...

No, listen to me. Everything I have done in my life has led to this. Every choice I've made.

I know.

I should be happy. People are jealous of my success. That I have you two. That we're here.

We should be happy.

Everything. Whether we wanted it then or not ... I convinced myself it was for the best. Because you were still there.

I know.

Did you always know?

I do now.

I don't know how to make this better.

Neither do I.

His thin bones under his skin prickled against my breasts, like joined to like in fragility. I held him as he cried.

Dec xx

My husband lies in our bed.

My son's room is unlocked for a change. How many hours I have spent looking at him while he was asleep, at his quiet beauty. When all the wanting of the day before had ended, and he needed nothing more from me. When he was mine alone, and I could enjoy him selfishly, and completely.

I thought it would never end.

Now he can lock his door to me, and a ritual has become a luxury.

His hair is on his pillow. His face is tranquil. The arm across the duvet is covered in fine hair. There are strips of muscle where before there was only skin and bone. When he smiles, now, the girls in his class notice.

He is flowering.

Our flight home leaves in the afternoon.

Three weeks in India, then back here.

How long have my husband and son been like this?

Was I too busy to notice, before, that they didn't need me anymore? I was indifferent to their indifference. I was to them as they were to me. I didn't even see my son changing from a stripling to a tree.

It is best that we remember the ones we love as they were. Before winter strips them of their foliage, leaving nothing but the bare brittle bones beneath.

The moon is on my son.

It's always the bloody moon.

She has woken up. She whines.

At least she still needs me.

We step outside.

3

NEED

Liesl

Spring 2020

'Liesl.'

'*Liesl!*'

She ignores his call. She will respond, eventually. But it won't do to let him think she is at his beck and call.

Must have discipline, Liesl thinks placidly. She closes her eyes, feeling the sun on her face. Her fingers play absently in the pot she's been working in, diving deeper into the moist loam. Soon, she thinks; soon, these flowers will be ready as well. Irises to join the cornflowers when they bloom in the beds she tends with such care. Little bits of the blue sky amid the green and red and pink. Something for the children on the street to run their hands through as they walk by.

'Liesl.'

More plaintive now. Less peremptory. A request, and not a command.

'Why don't you come outside,' she says in her gentle voice. She hasn't raised it; indeed, she never does: she knows he will hear her. He always does. Especially now, when there is nothing else to compete with. The trash has been picked up already. The school up the hill is closed because of the lockdown. Clearly there is no traffic. The only sound on their quiet street by the forest is birdsong.

'It is lovely and warm. Come outside.'

He comes out a moment later, irritably clutching his cardigan close at his throat. She looks at him in amusement, nods to the table on the generous balcony of their old home. A thermos of coffee is ready. He sits down with a thump. She pours him out a steaming mugful, watches him wrap his hands around the warmth.

'I wish you'd listen,' he says.

'I wish you'd keep quiet.'

He sighs and closes his eyes, his head back against the seat.

Liesl leans to kiss her husband's bald head, her lips cool against the liver spots.

'Were you in your pots again?'

'How can you tell?'

'I can smell the soil.'

'Isn't it lovely?'

He says nothing, his eyes still closed. But his face relaxes. She sits down next to him.

'I left the chalk out for the children. They enjoy drawing on the sidewalk.'

'Dogs pee there.'

'Hush. You didn't mind when it was your daughter doing the drawing.'

He opens his eyes at the memory. 'Forty years ago?'

'Closer to 50.'

'I was a different man then.'

'You're telling me.'

He chuckles.

They watch a woman walk by their home, her small dog on its leash. You can set your watch by her passage, Liesl thinks. The same times, every day. The same look on her face. Shut in her own world. What is she thinking?

'Where do you think she's from?' Liesl murmurs.

'Why don't you ask?'

'What if she doesn't speak German?'

Her husband grunts, closes his eyes again.

Spring came suddenly this year, but with great certitude. The path down from the forest is steep, Liesl's beds at waist height for those on the sidewalk. The woman below looks at the flowers blooming in their beds. She has taken to stopping this past week to savour the sudden show. She runs her hand along the side of a tulip, then looks up. Her face is almost guilty. Liesl doesn't want the unknown woman with the dog to feel that way. The flowers are for everyone.

'Lovely, aren't they?' Liesl smiles, her blue eyes crinkling. One might think they're the same colour as the flowers she loves so much.

Her voice is clear. There is no other sound. The woman below can hear her, no question.

She looks up at the old woman on the balcony without saying anything. Her lips move, but she says nothing, as if speech is unfamiliar. She nods, finally, and walks away.

Liesl stands on the sidewalk, her gloved fingers working among her beds. She wears a hat against the sun, a cardigan draped negligently over her shoulders. It should be cooler than it actually is, but Liesl is grateful for the warmth. She only has so much time left. The longer she gets with her flowers, the better. Far better this, that the blooming arrives early, than it be late. What would she do then? Especially now, with this new plague; sit at a window and see nobody walking by?

She sees, from the corner of her eye, the woman with the dog come out of the forest. She feels her indecision. Should she walk past the old lady? How much of a gap should she leave?

The woman steps into the street to pass. She checks for traffic, but there is none. She sees Liesl is watching her.

Liesl smiles, makes room on the sidewalk so the woman and her dog can stand next to her. Five feet away, but still facing the flowers. After a moment, the woman joins her, her dog sniffing at Liesl's feet.

'Do you like them?'

The woman looks at Liesl without saying anything.

'Do you speak German?'

The younger woman shakes her head slightly. It is not that she has none, the gesture suggests; but she doesn't have enough to claim any real knowledge.

'English?'

She nods, much more certainly.

'I'm afraid my English isn't very good,' says Liesl ruefully, hesitantly.

'It is very good,' says the other woman.

Liesl looks at her in surprise.

'Much better than my German, at any rate. I am sorry I don't speak it, yet.'

Liesl waves her hands, the gay print on her gardening gloves gleaming in the bright light.

'I should speak it,' says the younger woman. 'I live here.'

'Yes, but the sickness. The school in the village is closed, surely?'

The other woman nods. 'I am taking online classes. But my progress is … slow.'

'You can practice with me,' says Liesl easily. She cocks her head deftly, flirtatiously. She considers the other woman, then extends her hand for a knuckle bump. The other woman gives a small laugh, then returns the gesture.

'Frau ...'

'Liesl. Call me Liesl.'

'Liesl,' repeats the other woman.

Liesl smiles.

The moment stretches. Liesl waits, her hatted head still cocked, the sun brilliant in a bright blue sky.

Finally—

'Ahilya.'

It comes out as if from a bottle forgotten for years at the back of a closet. Gluey, gloppy, the syllables stuck together.

She has to say it again. For herself, as much as for Liesl.

'Ahilya.'

'That is your name?'

She nods.

'Ahilya.' Liesl savours the sound of it. 'It is nice to meet you.'

Ahilya turns and walks away.

Liesl watches her go.

So, she thinks, burying her fingers once more in her beds—

We are, all of us, alone.

'Is it time for you to speak to that foreign woman again?'

Liesl looks up at her husband peering down from their balcony.

'Your coffee is right there,' she says calmly. 'There's a roll on the table inside. Eat whenever you're ready, if you're hungry.'

'Heike hasn't called today.'

'She'll call when she has time.'

'Time? What else does she have right now? It's not as if she's working.'

'Why don't you call her then,' suggests Liesl.

He can't see his wife's face. She has bent back to her flowers, her hat shielding her from him as well as the sun.

He makes an irritated sound and withdraws back into the house. She looks up, notes the absence on the balcony. She feels the presence of the dog at her heel before she hears it.

'Hallo darling,' she whispers, stooping to tickle the dog behind her ear.

The two women smile at each other.

'Heike ...'

'Our daughter.'

Ahilya nods.

'You were listening?'

Ahilya shrugs.

'We haven't seen her since the lockdown started.'

'No, of course not.'

'It has been hard for him. Both of us. But especially him.'

'They are close?'

'Fathers love their daughters.'

'And mothers?'

'We know when to let go.'

'Do we?'

Both of them chuckle.

'Is she married?'

Liesl shakes her head.

She can feel Ahilya retreating, as if she fears having broken some sort of unspoken code.

Liesl waves it off. 'I don't mind you asking. As long as you do it in German.'

Ahilya assembles the sentence carefully before she releases it into the world. 'Does she have a ... man?'

'Why would it be a man?'

Ahilya laughs out loud. Liesl smiles. The younger woman notes the blue depths of her eyes. My god, she thinks, you must have been absolutely bewitching.

'We have no grandchildren,' says Liesl briskly. 'I wish we did. It would have made things easier.'

'For whom?'

Liesl turns back to her flowers. She is hiding eggs among them for the neighbourhood children. Easter is warm and sunny this year.

She does it every year, but this time, with the sickness, she has painted little messages of love on each one. A word or two, a doodled heart among the swirls of colour, a chocolate egg among the protein shells. Even if she can't touch the kids physically, have them stop at her door so she can give them something to eat she has made herself—this is something she can do.

'For the children?'

'And me.'

Ahilya nods slowly, but the old woman is still bending over her beds.

'Where are you from,' Liesl asks over her shoulder.

'India.'

'You've come a long way.'

'I really have.'

'What do people eat there?'

Ahilya's sour smile goes unnoticed behind Liesl's bent form. 'Perhaps I'll bring you something.'

Liesl looks up. 'I would like that. I don't think I've ever eaten anything Indian before.'

They sit one to each side of a table in Liesl's garden, fully five feet from each other. The trees around shade them from the sun. There is coffee, a cake that Liesl has baked, a Tupperware box full of sweets Ahilya has brought across.

Liesl makes her way painstakingly through the collection, breaking a little bit off each treat with the end of a spoon, popping it in her mouth with her fingers to consider it from every angle. She makes up her mind, positions two of them on her plate.

'These, I like.'

'And the rest?'

Liesl smiles. 'You think me rude?'

'I think you're honest. I don't particularly care for Indian sweets myself. They're too rich.'

'Did you make them?'

Ahilya is silent.

'You bought them from the store in the village?'

'You think me lacking?'

'I think you're pragmatic.'

To one side, through French doors open to the fresh air, lies a study. There are books, an old upright piano against a wall, flowers from Liesl's garden. On the piano, photos among the music. There is one, larger than the others; a man with his arm around a young woman's shoulders. Liesl sees what the younger woman is looking at and gets up to retrieve it. She puts it on the table between them.

The man is holding the woman close. She hugs him back around his waist. Her head is level with his shoulders. He is in a suit. She wears a dress, a sweater over it. Her shoes have a prim heel. Even in black and white, without the benefit of the blue in her eyes, the young woman in the photo is recognisable in the old woman across the table.

The couple look openly at the camera. They are secure in each other. They seem invincible.

'Your husband?'

Liesl sips her coffee.

'So handsome.'

'He was.'

'Tall.'

'Very. It was a problem, to begin with.'

'Why?'

Liesl mimics the act of craning up. 'All the things people warn you about before you get married ... Nobody mentions height.'

Liesl cranes up again, giggling, now, and Ahilya follows suit. A pantomime is playing out above. A pair of crows furiously attack a much larger hawk. They wheel in circles against the blue sky, the smaller crows taking it in turns to harass the raptor, till he flies away with an indignant cry.

'We can learn so much from birds,' says Liesl. Ahilya looks at her for explanation, but there is none forthcoming.

A young woman passes on the road to the side with her two children. The young boy runs in front, the smaller child laughs in his mother's arms. They stop at the chalk Liesl has left out, kneel to the sidewalk, begin to draw.

A hedge shields the garden from the street. The young family doesn't know it is being observed. Liesl watches quietly.

'You love children.'

Liesl nods gently. The children chortle as their designs come to life, the mother murmuring encouragement.

'Do you know them,' Liesl asks presently.

'I've seen them in the forest. We haven't spoken.'

'She will have a photograph like this with her man as well. We all do, don't we?'

The young mother laughs. She lifts her head, her hat tilts back, her sons frolic around her. Her face is aflame.

She is an angel.

'Perhaps you should meet her.'

Ahilya doesn't look at Liesl. She is still studying the woman on the other side of the hedge, her smile, the delight her little family are taking in each other.

If she were to meet someone new, what would she say? Aside from Liesl, nobody has even asked her her name this year, and it is Easter already. The engine is still rusty. She fears its fragility.

Ahilya speaks to perhaps two other people on this continent. What if the woman on the other side of the hedge is tongue-tied? What if she speaks no English, and her German is as bad as Ahilya's own?

Liesl leans across and pours more coffee into the quiet woman's cup.

'When you're ready, then.'

'You love your garden.'

It is not a question. Liesl stands, gloved hands on her hips, looking into her flowerbeds for enemies that must be eradicated. 'You have a garden as well,' she replies calmly.

'A small one.'

'Size is irrelevant.'

'I don't know what to do with it.'

'You have no interest.'

This is clearly true. The plants Ahilya cares about are inside her home. Pots and their upkeep are known quantities to those who have had their lives in apartments. Rooting in beds at the mercy of the elements is a different world. Drowned lettuce; rows of beans ravaged by snails; chillies put in to remind her of home laid waste by the shifting temperature gradients of this bland land—what would be the use?

'I never had any ... lust, for a garden.'

Liesl nods briskly, still peering at the bed at her feet.

'I wasn't raised with one,' offers Ahilya.

'Neither was I.'

Ahilya looks at her in surprise. Liesl sinks slowly to her knees, reaching for a weed she has seen.

'I thought ...'

'That I was born to this? A house like this one? A garden this big?'

Ahilya considers the older woman's bent form.

'When the war ended, my family ended up in a camp.'

One weed is followed by another. Then another.

'Where did you come from?'

'I was born in what had been ... What became Czechoslovakia.'

'The war ... WW2?'

The older woman twinkles up at her. 'How old did you think I was?'

Ahilya acknowledges this.

'Where was the camp?'

'In the Soviet zone.'

'The DDR?'

'That came later. But yes. There.'

'No gardens?'

'There was earth. We needed food. We grew things. Those first few years, we had to.'

Weeds Ahilya can't even see are coming out of the bed. Her dog noses about in the corners of the bed, looking for what is exciting Liesl's attention.

'I like the forest,' says the younger woman.

'You spend enough time in there.'

'My dog likes it too.'

'Of course she does.'

'The forest doesn't need me.'

'No. It just is. We can all be free in it,' murmurs Liesl. She holds up a hand. Ahilya offers her elbow so the older woman can lever herself up.

Then, she steps away again. Liesl looks at her, a faint smile at the corners of her mouth, in her blue eyes.

'I don't keep a garden because of my time in a Soviet camp. I don't eat my flowers.'

'Of course you don't.'

'They make me happy. What makes you happy, Ahilya?'

It must be nice to be old, thinks the younger woman. You can say whatever the fuck comes into your head. She bends to her dog to reattach her lead. It is time to go.

'I love the forest as well,' says Liesl calmly. 'I just don't walk up there as much as I used to. Not anymore.' She takes off her gardening gloves, wipes a hand across her forehead. 'May I come up with you, one of these days? There are things up there we can bring down for your garden. The forest won't miss them.'

Ahilya looks at Liesl.

'I have a bag. We can carry it between us. It won't be so heavy.'

Ahilya says nothing.

'I'll walk as quickly as I can,' says Liesl.

Ahilya knows the old woman is studying her. Obliquely, as she does.

'I promise,' says Liesl quietly.

Ahilya nods, finally.

'You'll see,' says Liesl. 'I won't hold you back.'

The sun decides to disappear the day they go up. Ahilya lets her dog off the leash. She runs up the path, looking back every so often to see where her two women are.

Ahilya finds it hard, at first, to walk as slow as Liesl has to. She feels unbalanced, off-kilter, as if she will fall over at this pace. Walking has its rhythm too, and she is walking to someone else's. It has been a long time since she had to make such an adjustment.

She is glad for the company though.

The church bells peal out. It is time for morning service. Not that the faithful collect under the eye of the priest, anymore. But those that are so inclined can dial up the service on their devices, or pass the time in quiet contemplation.

Sundays are quiet everywhere in this country. Aside from the church bells. The regulations don't apply to them.

'Are you religious?' Ahilya is curious.

Liesl looks sidelong at her. 'I save my kneeling for my flowers.'

Ahilya chuckles.

'Are you?' asks Liesl.

'I don't see the point, really. The benefits only kick in once you're dead. And the drawbacks ... "Don't do this, don't eat that" ...'

Liesl nods. 'My husband thinks he believes. He was raised in the church. When he hears the bells, they speak to him.'

'Is he praying right now?'

'Oh, he doesn't pray. He'll just sit. Be quiet. Think spiritually.'

Liesl looks at her. Ahilya expects the small smile of a joke shared in her eyes, but it isn't there. She is merely stating a fact.

'This is our problem, isn't it? Even when we believe, we do it tepidly.' Liesl sighs. 'We're either starting wars, or doing nothing at all.'

Ahilya looks at her in surprise, but the older woman has her eyes set on the top of the hill. Her body is bent against the slope and she is focusing on putting one foot in front of the other on the rough stones of the path, so as not to fall. They can no longer see the little cluster of homes at the bottom of the hill where they both live.

My god, thinks Ahilya; if she were to fall, what would I do?

'Do you really believe that,' she asks.

Liesl says nothing.

'Did you mean Germany? Or Europe?'

'Is there a difference? They're both invented.'

Liesl is straining, now, but they're almost at the top. 'Where I was born. Where I grew up. This place, where I'll die. One name, then another. One flag, then another.'

They are in a clearing, a tepee of sorts stacked in the centre with branches. Ahilya's dog scampers off into the bushes that are just starting to harbour secrets again. Liesl looks around, comes to a stop. She sits down on the trunk of a fallen tree. Her breathing is uneven, suddenly loud now that they're both still.

The trunk is long enough for them both to sit on, the requisite distance from each other. Ahilya waits quietly for the old woman to catch her breath. She reaches in her little bag for a bottle of water, starts to offer it to Liesl, but stops herself. She has already drunk from it. Liesl smiles, waves a hand. She isn't thirsty.

It is a companionable silence, now.

A rustle to the side draws their attention. It is just a bird, looking for something on the forest floor. A squirrel rushes across the clearing. Time settles.

'I could fall here.'

Ahilya nods meditatively.

'It is a good place to end things, is it not? To fade away in. So quiet.'

'Forests aren't really quiet, though.'

'No. You're quite right. They're just empty of the noise we make.'

'Is that what you like about them?'

They can see a bench in the distance through the trees, which are still mostly bare. A man is sitting on it, perched on one end. He has a flask of something with him. He seems to be waiting for someone.

Liesl's breathing is now back to normal. 'Do you know that man?'

Ahilya nods. 'His name is Nabi. He is always here at this time. His morning break, I suppose.'

Liesl acknowledges this. 'Nice man?'

'I barely know him.'

Liesl says nothing, waiting.

'He is Afghan. He speaks some Hindi. We've said hello.'

'You don't want to be friends?'

'He isn't short of female company.'

Liesl raises an eyebrow.

Ahilya grins. 'He is nice-looking. He seems gentle. His eyes are ... warm. There are always girls.'

Liesl laughs out loud, Ahilya's dog raising her head at the sudden sound. The cathedral hush of the clearing takes a moment to return.

'You don't have many friends, though. Do you?'

Ahilya flushes, but there is no judgement to flinch from in Liesl's voice. No sympathy to resent.

So, quietly—

'No. I really don't.'

'You have me.'

Ahilya looks up and smiles.

'Shall we return,' asks Liesl. 'I'm afraid I can't go any further.'

'The things you wanted to pick up for my garden?'

'Perhaps another day? There's no rush.'

Ahilya whistles for her dog. She helps the older woman off the trunk. They set off, the three females, down the hill.

They go up the hill every other day. Liesl's husband watches from his balcony as his wife strides off with her new friends. He starts his first cup of coffee when they leave, he'll be finishing his second by the time they return. An hour, more or less, that punctuates his morning, between all the other hours of doing nothing else.

He could help in the garden. But that has always been Liesl's domain.

He could walk in the forest. But he doesn't trust his footing anymore.

He would speak with his daughter. But she isn't sitting with him.

Not now. When he most needs her.

There are others like him in this little village; old people rattling around in big houses by themselves, now that they don't have offices to go to, now that their children are gone into their own separate lives. Now that the world is locked down. If a giant were to come and pick my house up and shake it, he thinks mordantly, what sort of noise would it make? Would I be the dried-up old seed inside that hits the walls and produces the sound and so sets the room to dancing? The thought diverts him. His view is of a row of maracas with sloping roofs and well-tended gardens. But the diversion is a short one.

He looks at his phone, yet again. It is too early for him to call, surely. Even if he were to talk to her for half an hour; once they were done and she had whispered 'I love you' before she disconnected; what, then, would he have to look forward to?

He had walked down the street the day before to the home of a man he had known his entire life. This man and he should have been friends. They were born within metres of each other, and only months apart. They went to the same school, worked for the same gigantic auto company that employed everyone they knew. They had retired the same year. They even belonged to the same clubs.

Their lives had followed the same trajectory as those of countless other men their age. Born of a war, delivered into ruins, setting their shoulders to a hulk that needed to be set rolling again; walking in lockstep towards a future those distant boys in that shattered land could never possibly have imagined.

But the truth was that they were neither friends nor enemies. Their relationship was marked with indifference, of a sort that comes with age and practice. Yet, he had walked down the street to meet this man whose life had raised not a ripple on his own.

He had stood in that man's garden and shouted his name. After what seemed an age, his wife had come to the door.

'Uli,' she said fretfully. 'I'm so glad you're here.'

'What's happened? Isn't Gerd home?'

'He's inside. He refuses to come outside. He refuses to do anything.'

'Does he know I'm here?'

'Of course he does. Wait.' She turned and shouted inside. 'Uli's here! Won't you come out?'

From inside, the silence of the tomb.

Her shoulders shook. She seemed close to tears. 'I'm so worried about him. He won't eat. He won't even bathe. He needs hours to get out of bed.'

'Your sons ...'

'They can't come, Uli. You know that. He just ... He says he doesn't want to live anymore!'

The unspoken thought was in the open.

'I show him photos of our grandchildren. My oldest will be thirteen this year. I told him, 'Don't you want to be at his birthday?' His thirteenth birthday, Uli. It's a big occasion.'

'Of course it is.'

'This will end, I tell him. Life will continue.'

'What if it doesn't?'

'Oh, Uli. Not you too. Don't say that. It has to get better.'

Uli: quiet, hatless, miserable in the sun. Desperately uncomfortable.

'It has to,' she insisted. 'It has to!'

He had wanted to reach out and hug this woman, this neighbour of half-a-century's standing, the wife of an almost-friend. At least to touch her on the shoulder, to let her know it would be okay. But he didn't. The rules were clear.

'No,' he'd said. 'You're right. The government's acted quickly. They're listening to the right advice. Things will be back to normal by summer.'

'Of course they will. Come back tomorrow, Uli? Please? I'll set up a table here for you two. A beer, maybe? Wouldn't you like that?'

He would love a beer with his oldest friend, said Uli. Then he'd left, shuffling back the way he'd come.

Assiduous as ever, is Uli. He has never passed a dirty dish in the sink without taking care of it. He has never left a magazine on the floor. He has never left a task uncompleted.

The walk back to his house had taken an age.

The cloudy sky had given him an excuse today. Surely Gerd's wife wouldn't expect him to walk down the street if the sun wasn't out? Surely she hadn't put the table out in expectation of his arrival? And for what? So he could bear the burden of lifting off her husband the shroud that he had chosen to take on before he was actually dead?

A young woman passing below hails him, hauling him back to the present.

'Hallo, uncle,' she shouts up with a smile. An old dog shuffles at her feet.

Uli's mood lightens. He smiles back. He knows this girl. He has known her since her birth. Her mother and his daughter Heike are childhood friends. He has always been an uncle to this girl, as he is to her mother.

'How are you,' he replies. 'It's been so long!'

'Just since Christmas. Not that long, surely?'

Before Christmas, thinks Uli. A different world. One without the sickness. My Heike was sitting at my table, eating the meal I made. But he doesn't voice the thought. He has learnt that time runs differently for younger people.

'What are you doing here?'

'Babysitting Nacho.'

'Parents away?'

'Trapped in Thailand.'

Uli rolls his eyes theatrically. The girl laughs.

'Your aunt is up the hill. She'll be back soon.'

'I know. I wanted to say hello to you.'

They grin at each other. They have always been friends.

'I'll come sit with both of you later. Safely. Is that alright?'

'Whenever you want, darling. We look forward to it.'

The girl waves as she walks away.

It is raining. The trees are in broader leaf now. They slope the moisture away from the three of them. As long as they stay under the trees, the rain is hardly more than a sound. The drops fall softly on the forest floor.

Ahilya's dog roots about under the leaves.

'Do you think she is more at home up here than down there? In your house, with you?'

'Who would feed her in the forest?'

'Isn't some part of her wild? At least a little?'

Ahilya looks at Liesl obliquely. But the old woman is intent, as ever, on putting her feet securely on the ground.

'Is it too wet?'

'Not yet. If there were to be a storm, yes. A slick root would end me.'

It is a simple statement of fact.

'Don't worry,' says Liesl. 'It won't get worse. We can continue.'

'You have a feeling for such things?'

'No more than anyone else. I've just seen it happen more times.'

Ahilya chuckles. 'I am glad I have you, Liesl.'

Liesl smiles gently.

'I am,' insists the Indian woman. 'When first I arrived, I was shy. Everything was new and I had no German. Then the sickness ending everything ... We only just came this past summer.'

Liesl nods. She says nothing of the 'we'. It is as if she hasn't noticed. 'Language is a problem,' she agrees. 'I only learnt English in my fifties. In the school in the village.'

'Did you learn a foreign language growing up?'

Liesl looks sidelong at her. 'I grew up in the DDR. What do you think I learnt?'

Of course. 'Is it still good?'

'My Russian? I don't know. I have nobody to practice with.'

Ahilya wonders if the old woman misses that other tongue. But she doesn't ask.

'Who else do you speak with, Ahilya?'

The question is posed gently, but it requires answering.

'There is a woman. She runs a bar up there.' Ahilya waves a hand up into the forest. 'She speaks English as well.'

Liesl nods again. 'I know her. Half ... Turkish?'

'Cuban.'

'Umm. Then?'

'There is an Indian woman of about my own age. We met before the lockdown. On the street. We recognised something about each other. We aren't friends, but we speak Hindi. It is ... nice.'

She pauses. Liesl waits for her to continue.

'She adopted me.'

'She needs you?'

Ahilya is silent. To say more would be to betray a confidence, she feels.

'What does she do?'

'She works at the municipal incinerator.'

Liesl raises an eyebrow, then nods. 'There is nobody else?'

Ahilya shakes her head.

They are at a crossroads of sorts. Wooden signs on the trees name the paths and where they lead. A bench sits to the side, still mostly dry. Liesl sits down with a sigh. A lone man on a bicycle whooshes silently by, lights and high-visibility Lycra vanishing quickly into the forest.

'Friendships aren't always equal.'

Ahilya knows this to be true. She feels a gust of wind where she stands, pulls her jacket closer at the neck.

'To be needed is important. At every age.'

Ahilya looks away, to where her dog is foraging by the side of a little brook that has sprung to life with this rain.

'Your family ...'

'They aren't here.'

'No. I haven't seen them in months.'

The rain patters down on the hood of Ahilya's jacket. The sound of it echoes in her head.

'That woman we saw,' says Liesl eventually. 'With the children. She may need us.'

'Why?'

'Her husband is abusive. He is supposed to have no contact with her and their children. But she worries about him.'

'How do you know?'

'People tell me things.'

I know they do, thinks Ahilya.

'This lockdown may not help her.'

'Won't it?'

'She thinks the authorities have too many other things to cope with. If he were to come, take her sons, perhaps ... What would she do? All the offices are closed. Who would she turn to?'

It is plausible.

'Is she from here?'

'Bosnia.'

'Her husband as well?'

Liesl shakes her head briefly. 'She met him here.' A pause. 'An animal.'

Ahilya notes the lack of inflection. She has no doubt the man's nature is as described.

'Especially at a time like this, Ahilya. It is good to be needed.'

'Love ...'

'Love is nothing without need.'

Ahilya closes her eyes and stretches her neck upwards, letting the gentle rain fall on her face. She has a question she must ask.

'Without need, then, what does love become?'

'Fondness. Affection. Indifference, in time.'

'Your husband ...'

'Really, really needs me.' The old woman smiles. She stands, Ahilya bending forward to help her up.

Are you still fond of your husband? Liesl sees the unspoken question in the other woman's dark eyes. She begins to laugh and so too does Ahilya, their merriment filling the dampening cloister, rain sloping down the ribs that hold up the vault of the darkening sky, soaking the giant beams. Then they're gone, the three of them, their passage lost in the sound of the rain.

'There's your foreigner again.'

'She's Indian.'

He grunts. She leaves to join the woman below.

He looks at the visitor, waiting patiently with her dog on the sidewalk. She has the good sense not to wave, he notes. He has ignored her before. She will avoid his eye, he is sure, but she looks up and holds his gaze calmly.

He nods stiffly. She does nothing.

From somewhere, he dredges up a smile.

It surprises them both.

The woman looks away.

He wonders if she will mention it to Liesl, who joins her now. Liesl bends to pat the dog, who cranes up to meet the gesture. They walk up the hill, Uli's eyes following them till they are out of view.

The sun is high and warm again.

'This weather is completely mad.'

'Isn't it? It feels as if it hasn't rained in weeks.'

'How will your flowers manage?'

'They're already struggling. I'll have to water them again this evening.'

'Don't you every year?'

'For a few days only. Never this early. Never so much.'

Ahilya lets her dog off the leash. The forest might be dry, but it feels wonderful. The leaves on the floor crackle under their feet.

'How old were you when you came?' asks Ahilya.

'Here? When I was a student. I came as part of a programme. I must have been ... eighteen?'

'Was it hard to come?'

'Very. Young people weren't encouraged to travel. Especially not here. It was a very hard programme to qualify for.'

'How did you find it here?'

'A different world.'

Delivered without inflection, again. It brooks no argument, invites no further questioning. Yet Ahilya presses ahead.

'Was it hard to go back?'

Liesl looks at her, the familiar flirtation pulling at the corners of her eyes and mouth. 'Who went back?'

Of course. It tickles Ahilya that she is walking with a defector.

'My parents suffered. They knew what would happen. They still told me to go.' Liesl's voice is gentle, still. 'There was a family, my mother's cousins. They had moved from the old country before the war. They were expecting me.'

'Did you ... run, alone?'

'There were two of us. Another girl and me. She died two years ago.'

'I'm sorry.'

'Why? She became a professor. Head of her department. She had a good man, three children, many grandchildren. She had a wonderful life.'

Liesl sighs, in its susurration a life lived in full and the weight of its memories; that weight, now that the story has been told, dispersed into the air.

'She was my best friend.'

You know what it is to run, thinks Ahilya. You know what it is to leave a home behind, all and everything in it.

I know what you have been.

Liesl sees it in her face.

'I, too, know what it is to be alone,' nods the old woman. 'I miss her every day. We only had each other, when first we came. Our parents, our families ... We didn't hear from them for years.'

'Did you see them again?'

'Twenty years later.'

'No.'

'When I went back, they were like strangers.'

What else would they be? They waved when you left as little more than a child, supposedly for a week; you return decades later a woman, a mother, countless unmet people and their stories behind you as your parents wait at their door—

Who dressed your hair that it looks so fine, thinks your mother;

Whose hands held your child when first she arrived, thinks your father;

How many shoulders has your head lain on, as the sun crept along your bed?

So many questions.

So much weight.

That is why people cry when they see each other after a long time, thinks Ahilya. The idea of bringing each other up to date is just too much to bear.

'Heike and Uli were with me. We drove there.'

'How did that go?'

'Heike loved it. They made such a fuss over her.'

'Your husband?'

'He never spoke of it again.'

The two women chuckle together.

'My mother died before the wall came down.'

'Your father?'

'He is buried here.'

In four words, the entire history of a promise made and kept.

Of course he is.

'This is where I'm from. Where I was born; where I was raised; they mean nothing to me. Not anymore.'

'Did you feel lighter?' Ahilya is curious. 'When did you know you didn't have to run anymore?'

'Oh, I never stopped running.' Her voice is light, but Liesl's face is averted.

No you didn't, thinks Ahilya. Running is what you know, deep in your bones. Even when the world thinks you're at peace, there you are, toes twitching, ready to go.

Liesl looks at her then, the familiar flirtatious look in her eyes. 'You think you know me?' she teases.

Ahilya blushes, then smiles.

'We make our peace with what we have. And where we are.' Liesl's voice is still gentle, but firm.

Ahilya is quiet.

'You disagree?'

'I don't know.'

'Making our peace with things is what we do.'

Ahilya shakes her head, again.

'You don't feel at home here,' says the older woman.

'If I were to die tomorrow, Liesl, nobody would know. Nobody would care.'

'I would care.'

'You know what I mean.'

The old woman says nothing, but her silence is eloquent.

'If nobody cares if I'm gone, was I ever really here?'

Through the trees they see the Bosnian woman's sons sporting in a clearing. The dog, who is now their friend, runs to join them. The boys are jubilant. The mother spies them and waves.

'My husband,' says Liesl. 'Men like him, of his age; they couldn't ever make their peace with the DDR. It was always a reminder of defeat.'

'In the war?'

'What else is there?'

Indeed.

'No matter your freedoms and your prosperity, there was that other place.'

'And you?'

They stand now on the edge of the clearing where the young family is playing.

'You get on with it. You manage. What else is there,' Liesl says again.

The cries of the boys trill around them.

'You must be needed, to belong to a place,' says the old woman; reflective, deflective. 'You must feel that you are needed.'

'You came to be needed here?'

'I still am.'

The young mother motions to them to join in their play.

'I think it is time you met her.'

They walk together towards the angel.

4

BURIAL

Harpreet

Spring 2020

'You think she'll come?' she whines.

'Of course she will.'

'Even in this rain?'

'The rain means nothing when you live here.'

'We live here, and it bothers us.'

'It bothers you.'

'If your hair were like mine, it would bother you as well.'

'True. You smell bad enough.'

She walks in. Her hood is up against the weather. She shakes off her umbrella, puts it in the bin. She is dripping wet.

Water slopes off her as she rubs her boots on the mat, takes off her jacket, shakes out her hair. She sees Ahilya and her dog and smiles.

Of course she was going to come. Where else would she be? Who else does she have?

Her name is Harpreet.

They are like this, these Sikhs. You can't tell their gender by their names. I could be a big hairy man, she laughed, telling Ahilya her name by the side of the road the day they met.

She is a small, pretty thing. But her hands are different. They speak of years of hard work.

They are gripped tight around her coffee mug today. Ahilya can see her veins. If she were to grip any harder, steam would rise from the skin.

That first day: she had bent, first, to Ahilya's dog. Dog and woman had taken to each other immediately.

'I love dogs,' she said.

'You should get one.'

'I can't look after myself, and I'll look after one of these?'

That laugh stayed with Ahilya. It was big, raucous, unexpected.

When Harpreet had called, the first time, Ahilya could have ignored the call; what do they have in common, after all, apart from being Indian women, and there are more than half a billion of those. She took the call because of that laugh.

Today, the dog is almost purring. Harpreet's hands have been busy in her fur. Her eyes are now closed.

'She's wet,' points out Ahilya.

'So am I.'

'She smells.'

'So do I!'

Now, with the dog at her feet, coffee in her hands—

'Bhainji—'

She calls Ahilya elder sister. Even though they seem to be the same age.

'—thank you for meeting me.'

'I called you,' points out Ahilya gently.

'Yes, but speaking on the phone is different. This is nice.'

'Yes, it is.'

'Especially with this sickness.'

'I know.'

'You know we're breaking the law?'

'She doesn't mind.'

They are in the Cuban's place in the forest. Ahilya's friend looks at them from behind her little bar.

'What if somebody were to see us inside?'

'Who comes up here?'

'How does she stay in business up here in the forest?' Harpreet looks up at the old beams. She studies the small windows, the huge empty fireplace, the antlers mounted above it. The rain hammers down outside. 'This place is creepy.'

'That's why we have it to ourselves.'

The owner walks across, a coffee pot in her hand.

Harpreet says something in a language Ahilya doesn't understand. She does it without thinking, then blushes, a hand across her mouth. She has forgotten herself, where she is: it is a language she hasn't spoken in a while. The half-Cuban replies with a smile in that unknown tongue. Harpreet removes her hand, her own grin spreading across her face. The two of them, hitherto strangers to each other, speak animatedly.

'Did you know she spoke Italian,' the bartender asks Ahilya finally, topping off her mug.

'I didn't know you spoke Italian.'

'I am an educated European. I have had boyfriends. I speak everything.'

They laugh. Harpreet watches the other two women quietly as they converse in their turn in an unknown tongue.

The owner notices her silence, turns to her, asks her something in Italian. Harpreet shakes her head. The owner nods in understanding and walks away.

'She asked me whether I spoke English.'

Ahilya knows Harpreet stopped at seventh grade in her village school. Of course she doesn't speak English.

But she speaks Italian.

She is full of surprises.

She sees the question in Ahilya's eyes.

In Hindi, the language they communicate in—

'I've been in Europe a long time.'

'Bhainji,' she says—

Her brother died the day before.

'Your brother? I am so sorry!'

Harpreet shakes her head. No, she doesn't actually have a brother. A full hand of sisters, yes, but her parents' luck ran out in this crucial instance. Just girls, one after another, till they finally turned off the tap.

The dead man was a friend. A close friend, like family. From the same village, their people connected over the generations. They had grown up next to each other, gone to school together. At one point, they'd even been mentioned as a match for each other, but their friendship had trumped that. She had sent him a rakhi every year, no matter where she was in the world. He was her brother. No less than that.

They would speak on the phone at least once a month. He would tell her of his growing family, how they were waiting to see their distant aunt.

He knew not to throw her childlessness in her face.

'He was a good man.'

'I am so sorry,' says Ahilya again.

He had taken ill about a fortnight earlier. It was nothing more, he said, than a cold. He had them every year around the time of the harvest. The chaff. The wind. Allergies. Nothing to worry about. Normal stuff for a farmer.

It got worse every day. A few days prior, he was raving in his bed, screaming obscenities, murderous threats at his children. His wife had called her in a panic, asking her help in calming him down.

They had gone to the hospital finally. The doctors asked his wife if he was an alcoholic.

'Of course he wasn't!'

They hadn't believed her. They wasted time thinking he was in withdrawal. Before they knew it, organ failure had set in. It was a small-town hospital. He was ventilated late, or perhaps wrongly. There was a lack of oxygen to his brain. He was alive, but not really. They took him off the ventilator and released him, so he could be taken home.

He died in the ambulance on the way there.

Ahilya reaches across and takes the other woman's hands in her own. Harpreet grips them as she did the coffee mug. Ahilya winces, but doesn't let go.

'Was it the sickness?'

'They didn't check. But what else?'

Ahilya squeezes her hands.

'I told everyone the government had it under control,' says Harpreet.

'Why would you think that?'

'They moved quickly, bhainji. They stopped all flights to India.'

'The sickness was already there.'

'Who knew that? Who?'

Ahilya says nothing. It wouldn't do to tell the stricken woman that she, Ahilya, knew. Along with half the world.

'I trusted them.'

Ahilya has little faith in governments, even less in the one running the country she has left behind. She stays quiet.

'We all did,' says Harpreet. 'Now look where we are.'

Where they are—

Ahilya looks away from the quiet desperation of the other woman, her eyes drawn to the old building's sweating eaves. The rain is a quieter presence, now. It seems to have eased, though the water still drips on the floor of the forest outside. She feels Harpreet's hands flex in her own, and she doesn't let go.

'I'd like to walk outside, bhainji.'

They get up, still holding hands. The three of them walk to the door, the Cuban watching quietly from her seat behind the bar.

'She is pregnant.'

'How do you know?'

'I can smell it.'

'She would have told me.'

'She may not have told anyone.'

'Does she know herself?'

'You'll have to ask.'

They are in the forest. The wet ground is soft beneath their boots. Closer to the floor lie the small saplings Ahilya had thought were dead. They have exploded into life and colour these past few days. Sightlines through the forest she took for granted are now being obscured. Her dog runs down one such alley, lost at once within the trees.

'I have something to tell you, bhainji.'

Ahilya nods silently.

'I missed my period.'

Ahilya raises an eyebrow.

'I checked. It wasn't negative.'

'Congratulations!' Ahilya is sincere, effusive. She knows what it means to the woman by her side.

Harpreet nods distractedly.

'Aren't you happy?'

'Of course I am! We've been waiting for so long. It is just ... This time, bhainji. The sickness. Is this the new world a child needs?'

It is your decision to make, thinks Ahilya. She believes this. She has lived her life by this. But she asks the question anyway.

'Have you spoken to your husband?'

'He doesn't know. Yet.'

No, thinks Ahilya. He wouldn't.

'I don't want him to know. Until I've made up my mind.'

Ahilya nods. Decisions needn't all be made in committee.

'So many injections, and peeing on sticks. So much unhappiness, bhainji. All that time, I thought two straight lines would make it all right.'

'Children don't fix things. It isn't their responsibility.'

'That's the whole point,' says Harpreet quietly. 'I'm responsible for this thing inside me. Not the other way around.'

The dog comes back to them. She has something in her mouth.

It is a dead chick. A little life that fell out of its nest and was extinguished on the forest's floor.

It is half-eaten.

Harpreet bends to the dog as Ahilya berates her.

'You think she understands you?'

'I know she does.'

Harpreet turns the little body over with her boot, then kicks it to the side of the trail. They use their shoes to rake a few leaves and dirt over the carcass. Deprived of her plaything, the dog stands disconsolately to the side.

'At least I know it can happen.'

'Getting pregnant?'

Harpreet nods. It worked this once. It could take again.

'My eggs are in the clinic.' She shakes her head at the memory. 'All that poking. They tell you it doesn't hurt.'

'Does it?'

Harpreet looks at her sideways. Then, abruptly, she grins.

'I have his sperm in the freezer.'

'What? At home?'

'Right next to the chicken breasts.'

Ahilya looks at the other woman open-mouthed. Harpreet's own mouth opens, her hand flies up to cover it. Then she explodes into laughter.

They both do, their howls of mirth rising up into the trees.

It rains again.

She comes up again to the Cuban's place in the forest. They meet outside the door. Harpreet is full of cheap sweet coffee from a machine. She can't face anymore.

No, she won't have a beer.

It is not that she doesn't drink. She enjoys keeping her husband company when they go out, when they are by a garden in the sun. When first he offered, they were in Italy, in summer, a week's wages in his pocket and a smile at last on his face; he felt, in some small measure, as if they could have a life in this new place. She had said no. Women like her didn't drink with their men. So what if the other women around had glasses in front of them?

But he kept asking. One day, she said yes.

'Keep him quiet, you know? I thought it would make him happy.'

'Did it?'

'It made me happy.'

'To make him happy?'

'Is there such a difference?'

Ahilya says nothing. Harpreet shrugs. There is no reason to drink right now. She would rather just walk.

The three of them, under the trees.

'It really isn't what you want?'

'It isn't that I don't want it, bhainji. Sometimes I feel that it is the only thing I have ever wanted. To have this other life inside me.'

'Then why do you hesitate?' Ahilya is gentle. It is for her to be supportive, and not judgemental. Try as she might, though, she knows how the question sounds.

'I have spent a life making other people happy.'

It is not an answer. It is not even a question. Yet Ahilya, educated, progressive Ahilya—she too has known the weight of those few words.

'Only we can give birth,' says Harpreet.

Ahilya is quiet by her side.

'Is that a good enough reason? Because I can, and my man can't?'

Ahilya sighs. 'It is your decision to make.'

It is cloudy today, but dry. The rain of the past few days is still apparent in the wet moss on the trees, the leaves on the path, the smell around them. A solitary jogger runs past. They give her a wide berth. Her 'danke' hangs in the air, breath made visible, long after she is gone.

'Have you told him yet?'

'Tell him what? I haven't made up my mind.'

'If you decide not to keep it ...'

'All the more reason not to say anything.'

'But he—'

'Is it my decision to make, bhainji?'

'It is always, and only, your decision.'

'Do you really believe that?'

'I do.'

'Then why is it important that he knows?'

Ahilya feels that she should know the answer to this. Her training, her legal practice and years of mentoring and advice, indeed, her entire life, should have equipped her with the right response to just such a question. But she doesn't have the answer. Or even an answer.

'He doesn't suspect anything. The last cycle was before the lockdown. It didn't take.'

Ahilya is puzzled. 'I thought ...'

'The doctor tested after ten days. It was negative. As it always is. Then I stop my meds and my period hits. Once it is over, we'll have sex. To make it up to each other.'

The forest is quiet around them.

'That's the only time we do it, anymore. After the crying is over.'

'At least you're still doing it.'

Harpreet shrugs. 'I really wasn't expecting to miss my period. He doesn't even know to ask. As far as he's concerned, we're waiting till the next cycle. Whenever that will be. With the lockdown, who knows?'

'Does he want you to go through all that again?'

'He wants me to be happy. If no longer trying will stop the crying, then that is what he wants.'

'Then he is a good man.'

'He is a very good man.'

There is a fork in the path, a bench to the side. They sit down on it.

'Nobody else knows?'

'Just you.'

He just wants her, Harpreet, to be happy.

'I could bury it inside of me. A little earth. Kick some leaves over it.'

It would be so easy.

'Sometimes I think I could just float up. That there is nothing holding me down, anchoring me to the ground.'

'It is understandable, that you don't feel rooted in this place.'

'Any place, bhainji. The things I've seen this past ten years ... And this sickness, now ... Why would it be different anywhere else?' Harpreet rubs her eyes. 'My brother's tribe was around him when he died. They could do nothing. What difference did it make to him?'

Her foot paws delicately at the ground in front of them. It is a tic, nothing more. But to Ahilya it seems as if she is searching for something. A remnant of another life, left behind by someone else. She cannot look away from the small, neatly shod foot as it scrapes and knocks against the earth.

'Is that why we have children? To be needed? Is that really all it is?'

Tap, goes her foot against the ground. Scrape. Pick.

'If I could just do one thing, bhainji, one thing that is for me alone, that is my decision. That means something. Is that so much to ask?'

No. It really isn't.

'Perhaps then I would truly be free. Of all that.' Her hand gestures vaguely behind her.

What does she mean, thinks Ahilya. Her husband's family? Her own? The life she has left behind in that distant country, or the place itself?

'All of it,' says Harpreet, quietly, without being asked.

Down one of the paths in front of them passes another small family. A young woman carrying a small child, and a little boy scampering at her heels. She looks up, sees the two women. She recognises Ahilya and smiles. Her sons wave animatedly. Ahilya waves back as the little group passes into the trees.

'They look so happy,' murmurs Harpreet. They can't see the family anymore, but the shouts of the little boys reach their ears till the forest falls silent.

'Everyone has their problems.'

'Even that sweet little family,' asks Harpreet disbelievingly.

'The forest swallows everything,' says Ahilya eventually.

Harpreet looks away.

'There are other people that need you,' says Ahilya. 'If you make yourself available.'

Harpreet tilts her head, but no more is forthcoming.

'When will your family return, bhainji?'

'When they can.'

Harpreet nods slowly. They hear Ahilya's dog in the forest, animatedly scraping at something she has found.

'Another dead bird?'

'Probably.'

The sun finally makes an appearance.

They meet by the bench. It is easy for her, Harpreet, to come straight there. There is a shortcut through the forest that she can take. It leads from her work to her home in the village. The bench is perfect.

The light filters gently through the trees. It is warm now. If they were to walk ten paces, they would be in a patch of sunlight so strong they could take their jackets off. They could lie there naked, as so many people do in this country. They could be there as their natures intended.

They settle on the bench instead. Harpreet has tea in a thermos. She made it especially for Ahilya. They savour it as they shed their layers.

'How is your brother's widow?'

'She has three young children to raise by herself. Her husband's land isn't in her name. She's not yet forty. So, yes. She's great.'

Ahilya flushes. Harpreet looks at her obliquely, then puts a hand on her sleeve.

'It is what it is, bhainji. She is strong.'

'If she isn't yet, she will be.'

Harpeet nods with feeling. 'Have you heard what they're doing now? Back home?'

Ahilya's phone has been full of so much bad news from India, she doesn't know what specific outrage the other woman is talking about.

'A cousin of mine works in Dubai. He got back on the last flight to India. He was quarantined in Delhi. Then he was quarantined at home. Bad food, terrible toilets. People crammed together.'

Ahilya nods.

'If he didn't have it when he came to India, he definitely picked it up in quarantine.'

They would both snigger if it weren't true.

'When he was finally released, the village wouldn't let him in. They said he might have the sickness.'

'What did he do?'

'What could he do? He spent the night under a tree, begging to be allowed to go home. At least it wasn't winter. He had fresh clothes in his suitcase. He washed under a tube well.'

'He's still there under his tree?'

'Three days he spent there. He finally negotiated a test from the district health centre. The doctor wrote him a note, and a constable from the station walked him to his mother's house. He's currently locked in a room next to the cattle.' Harpreet looks at Ahilya mordantly. 'He paid for that house. And those buffaloes.'

'You too have paid for things back home.'

Harpreet nods quietly.

'Are you worried that would happen to you, too? If you were to find a way to go home?'

'I know it would happen, bhainji. We're the carriers, aren't we?'

'Everything bad always comes from outside.'

'Unless it's our money. That's clean.'

'Spotless!'

'Maybe we should rub ourselves with it before we go out. To disinfect ourselves.'

They raise their cups to the thought, a quick cleanse with crisp currency to chase the infection away.

'How long will this last, bhainji?'

'Who knows?'

'A child in this uncertainty ...'

Ahilya nods in sympathy.

'How would I take her home? Where would she be from?'

'It won't last forever.'

'Do we really know that?'

No. We really don't.

'When first we came to Italy, bhainji, all those years ago, we told ourselves that it was for a better life. I mean, we had to say something to each other. Our lives were terrible. We had no papers. Dodging from flat to flat, sharing rooms with other people ... Not having a child was almost a blessing.'

Ahilya can see how that would be true.

'It was a relief to not hear people saying I was barren. Nobody says that to your face over here. Not even the Indians.'

Ahilya reaches to her shoulder. Harpreet doesn't look at her. 'I hate that word.'

Flat, without inflection.

'We got settled, finally. Everyone does. We got papers, entered the medical system. Learnt Italian. I met a doctor who found a way for insurance to cover my fertility treatments. There was no way we could have afforded those back in India. But here, in Europe, we had hope again.'

'That is why you have stayed?'

Harpreet nods pensively. 'My doctor in Italy referred me to a clinic she knew here, when she learnt we were considering a move. It all seemed to line up.' She pats her belly. 'And here we are.'

Indeed.

'That lady I see you with, bhainji. The old one.'

'Yes?'

'Is she a friend?'

Ahilya takes her time. 'I think she is.'

'She looks nice.'

'If you saw us, you should have said hello.'

'No, you were busy with each other. Walking right here.'

'When was that?'

Harpreet gestures vaguely. 'I was on my way back from work. I had a split shift.' She bends to the dog, to tickle her behind her ear. 'Your friend looks so peaceful.'

'Old people are that way.'

'Not in my experience.'

Ahilya looks sharply at the other woman, but she is still playing with the dog at her feet.

'Do you think she would understand me, if I gave it time?'

'My old friend, or my dog?'

Harpreet chuckles. 'In this case, I mean your dog.'

'I don't know. Why don't you ask her?'

'She needs us.'

'I know.'

'She needs you.'

'Oh, I know.'

'We all need to be needed.'

'Are you talking to me, or to her?'

'You are more alike than you know.'

They sit, today, on a little terrace behind the Cuban's bar. A casual visitor wouldn't even know it was there. You must step around the little kitchen, walk through a dark passage, and then you're on a bit of old wood with a few chairs on it, overhanging a little dip in the forest. The trees shield it from view, from passers-by, especially now that the trees are in leaf again.

If you sit long enough, says the Cuban, you're bound to see deer, the occasional family of boar, sometimes even a solitary fox. The wild animals run from people, but they ignore the house. They consider it part of the forest now.

'A hunter could cause some damage from this terrace.'

'I wouldn't let them. This place is a sanctuary.'

It truly is.

There are plenty of hunters' towers in these woods. The killers are welcome to climb those, says the Cuban, if the lust takes them. Let them bring their own coffee and booze for their cold vigils. They won't be getting any from her.

It is getting on. The shadows lie long on their little deck. In the forest below scamper a few unseen birds. The brittle beauty of their evensong is upon the air.

'Would you like a drink, bhainji?'

'A real one? What are we celebrating?'

'Nothing. I just thought it would be nice. I mean, it is evening. I would feel less guilty.'

'Why not?' Ahilya gets up to put in their order, reappearing in a moment with a bottle and two glasses. She pours the liquid for both of them.

They raise their glasses to each other. Harpreet reaches into a pocket and tosses a treat to the dog lying at their feet.

'Her, too?'

'She's part of the party.'

Ahilya nods. 'Nabi does that too.'

'The Afghan boy?'

'You know him, don't you?'

Harpreet shrugs, non-committal.

'Did you ever work together?'

'He offered to speak to his supervisor about working at the hospital. I decided I was happy where I was.' She grins. 'We're almost in the same trade, really. He guards them while they're dying. When they're done, they come to us.'

Her hand flies to her mouth, and then she roars.

'Oh please. Your place burns rubbish, not bodies. It isn't a crematorium!'

'It could be. But you're right. We do burn a lot of medical waste, though.'

'Is it laborious?'

'Not if you know what you're doing.'

'You do?'

'I've been there long enough. If you cut anything to the right size, I can get rid of it.'

'Anything?'

Harpreet smiles over the rim of her glass.

The silence settles around them. This deep in the forest, there are no cars, or construction, or other people. The dog settles in to the sun-warmed wood. There are blankets heaped to one side if it were to get cool. The two friends sink deep into their chairs, their faces to the trees.

Happiness would be an option, thinks Ahilya. If this were all there was.

'It isn't so bad, is it?'

'What?'

'This place.'

It could be worse.

'You can make your peace with any situation. Every woman I've ever known has had to.'

Ahilya can only agree.

'We could be happy here. The two of us. We don't need anyone else.' Harpreet looks sidelong at the woman next to her. 'My daughter and I; when she is grown. This would be a good place to set her free in. No?'

'Daughter?'

'I think of her like that.'

'Then you're leaning a certain way.'

Harpreet smiles and shrugs. 'We could only ever be friends here, bhainji. We could never just be sitting next to each other like this, having a drink, back home in India. Could we?'

Ahilya nods quietly. It is true, even though she wishes it weren't so.

'I mean,' says Harpreet, 'where would we even meet? A woman like you, and someone like me? I would be working in your home.' She closes her eyes. 'Perhaps this is where I was supposed to end up. A job, a good man, an old age with each other to look forward to in this place. Why would this new thing make it all better?'

Why indeed.

'We all have to die, eventually. What difference does it make where it comes?'

None at all.

'I would like to mark the occasion, though.'

'Aren't we?'

'Oh, it hasn't happened yet. I haven't even made up my mind. But if I decide to; after it is ... done, I'd like to have a ceremony.'

Ahilya says nothing. It isn't her place.

'I could just throw a few things in the furnace at work. You know. A list of names we drew up. Things like that.'

'Harpreet, please. Not there.'

'No, of course. You're right. Perhaps a fire here. In the forest.'

That would be more suitable.

'Will you do another cycle? If you decide that way? When all this is over?'

'I'll cross that bridge when I come to it.'

Ahilya nods. The idea of a bonfire in the forest is an engaging one. 'What would you put in it?'

'The fire? There is so much to throw away.'

Yes, thinks Ahilya. There really is.

'You're welcome to bring your own things to toss in.'

A doe pokes her head shyly out from behind a tree, then steps into plain view. Her fawn follows behind, picking daintily over the forest floor to his mother's side. His mother's ears flick this way and that. Her eyes turn to the terrace, where the two women sit. They eye each other quietly.

The doe bends to the ground, browsing gently through the debris. Her fawn, secure by her side, follows suit.

They need fear nothing here.

5

TEA

Nabi

Spring 2020

This is where men belong.

In the sun, with fruit in their hands.

Nabi looks up from the bench where he is sitting. The snow of the previous weekend has melted away. He had worried that the early flowers would have wilted, but they have survived. Indeed, they are thriving. The jacket he had on earlier lies next to him. It seems that spring has finally come to his corner of Northern Europe. Even if the trees around him are still naked; even if he knows that he will need his hat and gloves when he walks home that night; the promise of warmth is in the air, and Nabi welcomes it.

The hospital where he works is behind him, through the winter-thinned woods. Across from where he sits the forest continues down to the small town at the bottom of the hill. Where he lives.

He comes out here every day. Rain, snow, heat or cold make no difference. He walks up the hill on his morning break to the bench by the narrow lane that runs through the forest. Walkers, runners, the occasional cyclist would have gone by in days past, nodding briefly to the man they had learnt to expect eating his fruit to the side.

Before the sickness.

Now the district hospital is full, and he is working double shifts. He appreciates the money, but misses the time he previously had to himself. The stream of runners and walkers and cyclists has slowed to a trickle as well.

His mask hangs on his neck. A pair of rubber gloves he forgot to throw into the bin lie on his jacket. He stretches his neck up, bends his head back, cracks his shoulders diligently. His pause isn't long. He has learnt to use it well. His black hair gleams as he bends this way and that.

A sound comes to him, distinct from the birdsong. It is the laughter of young children. He frowns. The playground in the clearing across the lane is roped off, like every other Spielplatz in this country. Have these kids ignored the safety warnings? Do they want to end up in his care?

Then he sees them. A young mother who comes up the hill with her two children. She is like him—she ignores the weather. What is important is to be outside.

He knows the family. He has helped them in the past.

One child is small enough to be in his mother's arms. She carries that one everywhere. The other trails behind her. She never hurries him as he explores this way and that.

She always smiles at Nabi, at whoever is passing. He has never seen her be short with her children.

She is made of patience.

They are sitting in a clearing between the trees. The sickness is in the hospital to one side and in the village to the other, but up here, her little family has the bare forest to itself. Her son runs this way and that and the young child is feeling its way on its still unsteady legs. There is a basket in front of the mother full of treats for her children when they tire of their play.

Nabi looks at the orange in his hand. He sighs.

Where is she?

She is still wearing her heavy jacket.

He first noticed her when the illness began curtailing people's daily lives. As more and more people retreated behind their doors, aside from the young mothers, the ones that continued to walk up the hill fell broadly into two categories.

Those that couldn't do without the exercise. And those with dogs.

He knows the old dog shambling by her side. He would come up at this same time before the sickness as well, mostly with a pleasant-faced woman who used the walk to smoke, occasionally with a tall taciturn man who would nod to Nabi in passing.

This young woman is new. But she is regular.

He likes the fan of hair around her face. Her eyes contain the potential to smile. She is younger than he is, and he isn't yet thirty. She walks with an easy athleticism. She wears leggings. When the jacket is shed, her shape will be revealed.

Her shape will be to everyone's taste, he thinks wryly. Not just his.

Her dog notices him first and stops to sniff at his feet. Nabi feels in his pocket for the biscuit he has put there, and offers it to the old beast.

He snuffles at Nabi's outstretched hand for a long moment, then takes the treat. Only then does Nabi look up.

'Danke,' says the young woman briefly.

'Better him than me.' Nabi pats his belly with a smile.

She nods and walks away with the old dog, the sun above, the trees to either side.

Nabi looks after her, eating the last of his orange.

From down the hill comes the sound of an ambulance making its way to the hospital.

From across the path comes the sound of the children, happy and gay.

He quietly gathers his things and turns down the hill.

At least she didn't pull the dog away.

His comfort lies in such small things. The day had been hard. Every case they had at the hospital wasn't linked to the sickness. But the sickness itself lay like a shroud over it.

The sickness has a smell, he tells his brother over their daily video call, as he makes dinner that evening.

It smells like disinfectant.

Every hospital smells like disinfectant, scoffs his brother in distant Afghanistan.

'Not this much. It isn't just on the floors and the beds. It is on my hands. In my nostrils.'

'It could be worse,' says his brother. 'You could have a beard like me. Do you know how hard it is to shake a smell when it's lodged in there?'

Nabi laughs, fingering his closely-shaved cheek.

'It sounds bad over there,' says the other man hesitantly. 'Europe is struggling. Is your job safe?'

'I work in a hospital, brother. I just became the most valuable man on the planet.'

He wants his brother to smile, but the older man just looks away.

'I'll continue to send money. Don't worry.'

'We appreciate the money, Nabi. But it is so dangerous ... What if you get sick? Is it worth it?'

Nabi eats his solitary dinner by the window that night. His view is of a little lake ringed by trees that flamed into colour this week. It made him laugh when first he came, to hear the locals call that paltry stretch of water a 'sea'. Now, he thinks of it by that name.

Children should have been playing in the little playground across the lake, but it was closed as well. Geese fluttered to a halt in the water. They too were migrants, in transit, on their way home from someplace else.

There had been springs back home when his father and elder brother had hunted birds such as these. After the long months of winter, there had been nothing else left to eat. Those were months when a view such as this, dinners such as the one he was eating, would have seemed very distant. Even otherworldly.

He had dodged and lied, sheltered in strange lands, paid money to unscrupulous people, to finally be here, in this new world.

He had learnt a foreign tongue.

Nabi strokes the orchid he keeps in the window, whispers in the ears of the young blooms he has put in the flowerbox outside, all the while watching the family groups make their way around the lake. The isolated singletons keep their mandatory distance.

1.5 metres. Almost five feet.

If you're alone, thinks Nabi—

Five feet may as well be a mile.

She comes every day.

The dog stops at his feet and sits, waiting for his treat. Nabi knows his name is Nacho. He gleaned as much from the pleasant-faced woman who walked him before the sickness. He wonders about her and her silent partner. They hadn't passed through his hospital. He would have seen them.

'Hallo,' he whispers in the old dog's ear. He plays with it, its fur as silk to the touch. The dog sighs in contentment, rubbing his head against Nabi's hand.

His human watches quietly. Nabi concentrates on the dog. He has studied her hair as she walks away every day. It isn't quite blonde, but neither is it dark. It reminds him of the camp in Pakistan where he had spent one miserable year, waiting for his agent to put him on a ship. There were occasionally women who came by, local Pakistanis who were volunteering, reporting, 'experiencing'. They would pay money for their hair to have the colour this girl had been born to. Some of the men affected that colour as well.

The thought makes him smile.

'My dog makes you laugh?'

'He makes me happy.'

'Then he is of use in this world.'

'Some things don't have to be useful. Nacho is among them.'

'You know his name?'

He looks up at her. 'The lady who used to walk him earlier ...'

'My mother.'

'Ah, yes. She told me. I've been coming here every day since I started working at the Krankenhaus.'

'You never miss a day?'

'Not yet. You could set a watch by my break.'

She smiles, finally.

'My name is Nabi. I would shake your hand, but the sickness ...' He shrugs eloquently.

She nods, still smiling.

She walks away.

Before the sickness, when he had a few hours to kill, he would have arranged to meet a friend in the little mall nearby. A set of brothers from the same part of Afghanistan as him worked in a kebab shop there. The Kurdish owner was indulgent. He enjoyed his employees having their friends sit there and talk things over while eating their lunches and sipping their tea.

'It makes my place look busy,' he had told Nabi once. 'And you aren't sitting for free. You always eat.'

But things are different now. The mall is still open, but only because it has a supermarket and a drugstore. All the other stores are closed, save a few takeout eateries. The bustle is gone, and the mall is revealed for what it is, a temperature-controlled box with discrete compartments, most of which are now shuttered.

He knows a few of his friends congregated here in the early days of the sickness. They messaged each other to meet at one or the other takeout place, as if by accident. They would sit at adjoining tables and sip their coffee and they would have their social time.

But Nabi works at the hospital. He knows and respects the rules, and he refused to meet the other men. But he worried over the information he had been given about their movements. Was it enough that he didn't go himself? Should he have done more than tell his friends that they weren't just breaking the law, they were endangering themselves and their families, at least the ones that had them?

Should he have reported his friends for meeting as they did?

His dilemma only lasted a few days. Security caught on and moved them along and notices were posted. Finally, the tables were cordoned off. Tape was draped over the chairs.

He has come to the mall today because he has nowhere else to go. The day has been cloudy, and the sea grey. This meagre mall is the only public indoor space that is still open.

He walks past the empty storefronts. One shop, a lingerie outlet, has left its wares on display. Beside it is a travel agency, pictures of pristine Aegean and Turkish getaways still in the window. Nabi looks at the photos of those impossibly blue seas, the spotless white houses, the immaculately clad and smiling people. The prices make him purse his lips.

'Nabi, right?'

He turns around in surprise. She has stopped the requisite few feet away.

'You like women's underwear?'

He doesn't know what to say.

'For you, or a ... friend?'

He blushes, before nodding at the photos of the travel experiences.

'I know. I'm just teasing you.'

'What are you doing here?'

'What else is there to do?'

He shrugs. 'Perhaps I should be studying the underwear. There's more chance of me finding someone to give it to. I'm not going to any of these places soon. Nobody is.'

She bends her head to one side. 'Are you single?'

He nods.

'How would you go about meeting someone at a time like this,' she wonders.

He smiles. 'Would you like a coffee? Something to eat?'

The lone man Nabi knows to be Vietnamese looks up from his phone in the 'Chinese' restaurant across the central passage.

'I don't drink coffee,' she says. 'And I just ate. I'm here to walk it off.'

Nabi nods.

'I drink tea, though.' She smiles, and it seems to Nabi that the mall they are in isn't quite as empty as it had been moments before. Thus, emboldened—

'The tea here is undrinkable. But if you walk Nacho tomorrow morning, I'll bring you some I've made.'

The birds are in fine voice the next morning. The usual blackbirds are out, and the finches. Nabi likes listening to the birds, identifying top, middle and bass-notes, trying to tie them to the birds themselves. The cry of the raptors, the raucous crows, the constant rhythm set up by the woodpeckers running under it all. He could sit, he feels, for hours; just like this, his head bent back towards the tops of the trees, his eyes closed, soaking in the song and the sun.

He could be anywhere, he thinks hazily. Even on the hill behind his old home in Afghanistan. The urgencies of this new world are as air, as long as he is up here on his break.

The dog's muzzle feeling for his hands shakes him awake. She stands at the end of Nacho's leash.

He has made sure to sit right on one edge of the bench. He indicates the rest of the seat with a flourish. She laughs and sits down at the other end.

'Did you bring a cup?'

She reaches into her jacket and withdraws a small mug. He pushes the full thermos towards her, along with the packet of wipes. She helps herself, holds up her mug. 'To the sickness.'

'An end to it, you mean?'

She shrugs.

He raises an eyebrow, and then his mug.

'How long have you been here,' she asks.

'In Europe? Five years. Three years here.'

'Are you a doctor?'

'No. I clean. Run errands. Help the doctors and nurses. That sort of thing. When my German is ready, I'll try and get a nursing certificate.'

'You already speak well.'

'Not as well as I should. I need to belong here.'

'It is better than I would be in your language.'

'Do you know what my mother tongue is?'

'No.'

'Dari.'

'Where are you from?'

'Afghanistan.'

'Ah so.' She waves around herself in a gesture that encompasses both ownership and grace. 'Welcome.'

They both laugh.

She had been visiting from Berlin. She is a student of economics. It made no sense to go back there when the sickness came along. Her university is closed, her friends are indoors. Her social and educational world is going to be online, and she can do that from here as well.

'Do you miss it?'

She shrugs again.

'You're a long way from there.'

'Not as far as you are from Afghanistan.'

Fair enough, thinks Nabi. 'Do you like the tea?'

'It's absolutely delicious. What do you put in it?'

'Cloves, cinnamon, pepper, ginger. Cardamom as well. It's a family secret.'

'You'll have to show me how to make it.'

'After this is over ... Sure. Till then, I'm happy to make it for you.'

She raises an eyebrow. He hastens to explain.

'I make it every day, anyway. And I come up here to drink it. If you like, if you're passing, join me.'

'The weather is supposed to be good this week, right?'

'No rain at all for another two weeks.'

'What? I'll just have to carry my mug every day, then.'

'If it's too warm for a jacket, where will you put it?'

She smiles as she gets up. 'Come on, Nacho.'

He watches her prepare to leave.

'Mia,' she says.

'I'm sorry?'

'My name is Mia.'

Mia, he says, the word quiet and airy in his mouth, as she walks down the hill.

'Is it still cold, brother?'

'The valley is dry, now. But the mountains are still white. I don't think it is finished for the year. There will be more snow.'

'The herders haven't gone up yet to their pastures?'

'There is still time for that, Nabi. You know that.'

'I do. I just miss it.'

'I know. What is it like there?'

'Warm, now. Well, the entire winter was warm. The lake didn't even freeze.'

'That must have been nice.'

'No, I miss the cold.'

'Better you than me, Nabi. I don't have hot water out of the tap whenever I want. I don't ever want to feel cold again.'

'I know, brother.' Nabi wants to reach out to his elder brother, to hug him, to hold him tight against the snow he knows will return.

His elder brother smiles, shrugging it off. 'Tell me what you see, Nabi.'

'They're barbecuing in the house next door. It is that warm. I can smell the meat grilling.'

'Oh, how lovely. Is that the family with the three daughters?'

'Yes. The Croatians. The father cooks. He drinks and sings while he's grilling. It is wonderful to see.'

'Record his singing if you can, and send it to me?'

'I will.'

'You're a fine cook, Nabi. You have a barbecue too, don't you? On your balcony?'

'I do.'

'Make something nice for yourself.'

'What is the point of making an effort if you're alone?'

'So what will you eat?'

'Whatever is lying around. I have yesterday's rice. There is some chicken in the fridge. I'll fry some frozen vegetables in a little butter.'

His elder brother smiles again into his beard.

'What?' asks Nabi.

'It sounds like a feast to me.'

The forecast hadn't lied. The weather is fine. So fine, in fact, that Nabi feels warm as he takes his morning break. He stops bringing his heavy jacket up the hill; then he sheds his sweatshirt; finally, he waits for her in a t-shirt.

She comes up every day, the dog on his leash, a mug in her hand. She has shed her layers as well. She sits at her end of the bench. In the time it takes to drink two mugs of tea each, they talk.

There is a quiet curiosity about her that he responds to. She doesn't just ask questions to be polite, or to glean information. He has known those questions, and he has had his fill.

She wants, he feels, to know.

He points people out to her as they pass.

A silent woman with dark hair walks past with a little dog. The dog stops to say hello to Nabi, who has a treat in his pocket for her as well. The dogs clearly know each other. They sniff the other in a desultory way. The waiting woman nods almost imperceptibly at Nabi, before she pulls her dog away.

'She's Indian.'

'Really? How do you know?'

'We spoke a few times when first she came. She thought I was Indian too.'

'Do you speak Indian?'

'I speak some Punjabi. It is a lot like Hindi. We communicate.'

She looks at him.

'They are both Indian languages,' he explains.

She nods. 'How did you learn it?'

He tells Mia of the Sikh shopkeepers he had known in his old home. The son and he had been friends. That distant man and his family had taught him Punjabi. Even though they spoke Dari to each other, the Sikh family had remembered the old tongue, and passed it on to the young Afghan next door. That language had helped him navigate his time in a camp in Pakistan.

'I was always curious about other places. Other people. When they moved in, I made friends immediately.'

'I didn't think Afghanistan was that sort of place.'

'The kind where you have neighbours? Or where you befriend them?'

'I don't mean to offend you.'

'I don't mean to take offence. I am sorry.'

'You shouldn't be, when it is my fault. I know nothing about you. Or where you're from.'

At least she is making an effort, thinks Nabi. She is sitting with him on this bench while every single person on the planet has turned away from everything and everyone else.

It isn't even Mia's effort to make. He is in her country, which has taken him in. Why should any person here give one single solitary shit about the world he has left behind?

Instead, he tells her about the woman walking down the hill.

'She has a husband. A son. They arrived last year, at the end of summer.'

'Where is the rest of her family?'

'I don't know. I saw them a few times last year. Walking together, going up to the beer garden. Occasionally walking the dog. But I haven't seen either her man or her son since the New Year.'

'Maybe she killed them.'

'Indian women don't do that!'

'German women do?'

Their laughter rises through the trees.

It would be easier if he still had access to other people.

His colleagues in the hospital are no help, anymore. The ordinary camaraderie is still there, to a degree; they are in it together; but now the fellow-feeling is filtered through masks.

He has never been a smoker, but he enjoyed standing outside, rain or shine, as his co-workers took their breaks and talked over the news. Most of the others doing the work he did were immigrants as well. Afghans, Filipinos, Syrians; Europeans from the less privileged parts of that continent. They took comfort in each other's stories of their new lives.

Now, everything is different. They are surrounded by sickness and consumed with stress. When they are free, there is no hanging around the hospital, or with the other workers. Escape is paramount. Get away, go home, scrub the contagion off yourself.

It would be easier if Mia weren't the only person he was talking to through the course of the day. His solitude makes everything heavier than it needs to be. He worries that the weight will scare her away.

Who will he speak to if she disappears as well?

'How long has it been, Nabi?' asks his brother.

'Since I left? Six years. Almost exactly.'

Six years since last I saw my brother, he thinks. Six months before that of finding the agent, selling the land, raising and paying out the money the family couldn't afford to do without. So he could set sail for a distant world where things would finally be better. At least for one of them.

Six years of additions to his family back home. Subtractions, too. There were people from his past that he would never see again. Not in this world.

'Of course. It was spring then as well.'

'You'll see me soon, brother.'

'I know, Nabi. My son wants to meet his uncle.'

'I want to meet him. As soon as my papers are ready, I can start the process for all of you.'

'There is no rush. When my children are old enough, we will see. It is enough for now that you are there.'

'We have discussed this. I should begin the work now, so you will have the option when the time comes.'

'Hasn't this sickness stopped all that?' asks his brother pacifically.

'I don't think so. The country must run. All those bureaucrats are still working. Even if it is from their homes.'

'Do they ever think of us, Nabi? Or are we just names to them?'

'I don't know, brother. The ones I've met have always been kind.'

'I suppose there is nothing to separate us from each other. Our stories; your story: how different is it from the next person's?'

The indifference, real or imagined, of his adopted home to the people coming into it, was a conversation he has had with his brother before. To Nabi, who is grateful beyond measure for having been taken in, it doesn't really matter.

'They owe us nothing, brother. Yet, they house and feed and teach us.'

'They tax you too.'

'Good. It makes me feel like I am giving something back, finally. That I am not just a refugee anymore.'

'They have taken enough, Nabi.'

'This country? What has it taken from us? It never burnt our villages. Never bombed our schools.'

'But they are rich, and we are poor.'

'That won't change. Someone will always have to be rich, and someone poor. Otherwise why would people work for one another? This country took me in. We're square, as far as I'm concerned.'

His brother laughs. A sound behind him draws his attention, before he turns back to his phone. 'Your nephew has a cold. A bit of a cough. Fever.'

Nabi is shocked. 'You didn't tell me! Have you had him checked?'

'Check where, Nabi? I can't take him to Kabul. Besides, who is going to infect us up here? Nobody comes from the outside world during winter. It is just a cold.'

Nabi doesn't sleep that night for worry about that distant boy he has never met, yet loves with all his heart. He tells himself that he is being silly. His brother is right. How would the sickness reach their remote home?

The thought that finally brings him out of bed, conceding that there will be no sleep after—

He, Nabi, made it out. Why couldn't a virus, a thing that needs neither visa nor agent, get in?

'You look tired today.'

'I didn't sleep well.'

'I don't blame you. This is a strange time.'

'The strangest.'

'You must have seen some odd things, though.'

'I'm sorry?'

'Your frame of reference is different from mine, Nabi. I have never known anything like this.'

He doesn't know what to say, so he keeps quiet.

She reaches into the space between them, her hand patting the air, as if she wants to reassure him. But touching another person has become a memory for both of them and her hand falls short of its target.

'You won't tell me unless I ask, I know. But your journey here; being a Flüchtling ... I have a friend in university. A Libyan. The tales he told us of coming across ... Sometimes I wish the world would end.'

'What good would that do?'

'So we can start anew. From zero. Whatever we do, it has to be better than what we have now. Don't you think?'

Nabi cracks his shoulders. He is unconvinced that there is a world anywhere where there wouldn't be poor people in boats crossing the open sea in hopes of a better life. His opinion, shaped by the things he has seen, is that only rich people want poverty itself to end. Poor people mostly just want their poverty to end. When they aren't poor, anymore, is when they can start thinking of the lives of others.

But it is a thought he feels too tired to articulate, his otherwise serviceable German entirely unequal to the task. He doesn't want to risk an argument either.

'Your mother,' he says. 'Your father. I haven't seen them in a while. Are they well?'

She looks at him sideways. 'They're fine.'

'I was just used to seeing them walking Nacho.'

She laughs. 'Would you prefer them sitting here and sharing your tea?'

'No! I mean, they are welcome. I was just wondering ...'

'They're not here. They're in Thailand.'

Nabi nods. It is a story he has heard from others, of people left stranded outside when the borders closed.

'They had made plans to go before the sickness was known. When the first reports started coming in, they considered cancelling. But you know how quickly things moved. The information changed from day to day. When they finally made the decision to go, they had no idea they'd get stuck there.'

'Good thing you were here.'

'Excuse me?'

'For Nacho.'

'I came down for that reason. He's so old now. We thought it best that he stays at home, where he's comfortable. Instead of kennelling him.'

'Do you speak to them?'

'Every day. More than I would from Berlin.'

'Are they comfortable?'

'They're warm. Their view is of the sea. The bar by the swimming pool is still open. I think they'll manage.'

Nabi laughs. 'Do you wish you were there?'

'I can't afford it. It is better I am here, eating their food, keeping Nacho company. Spending their money instead of my own.'

What a privilege, Nabi thinks, to be stranded abroad and regard it as an inconvenience. A beach for him is still something to run across quickly, before the immigration officers swoop. Now the papers that save him from their scrutiny are in his wallet and on his phone. He can go where he wants. Or he could have, before the sickness.

But even if he had the freedom of movement; even though he has the money now—who would he go and marvel at the ocean with? Who would share that first moment, would understand what it meant for a man such as he, born and raised a thousand miles from the nearest sea, to have the salt waves lap his feet? Where was the family he would build sand castles with?

Is this depression, he thinks. The staff at the hospital are constantly being warned about it, told to self-monitor for its deleterious effects. Depression and its cousins are the enemy, just as much as the sickness itself.

You must keep talking, they are told.

Talk to whom, thinks Nabi. What of those of us who are still alone? Who do we talk to?

'Nabi?'

'I'm sorry, I was just dreaming. It is so lovely and warm.'

'It is mad, this weather. If it weren't for the sickness, everyone would be outside.'

'If it weren't for the sickness, you wouldn't be sitting on this bench.'

'True. Every small thing changes everything else.'

'I'm glad someone is drinking my tea.'

'I'm glad for your company, Nabi.'

He blushes and looks away.

'I mean it. I'm alone at home. I can't meet my old school friends, and they have their own lives anyway. You're the only person I have any contact with. Aside from the grocery clerks and the ladies at the bakery.'

Nabi looks back at her.

'I don't look forward to meeting them,' she says. 'But I do enjoy sitting here and drinking tea with you.'

'Thank you,' says Nabi, from his end of the bench.

'No. Thank you.'

'Why haven't you met anyone, Nabi?'

'What makes you think he hasn't?'

'He would tell us.'

'He's allowed to keep things from his brother.'

'I'm not talking about you. He would tell me.'

Nabi smiles at his sister-in-law. She is right. He has always confided in her, ever since she came as a young bride to their home.

She is sitting on a chair while holding the phone. His brother stands behind her, brushing out her glossy black hair.

'It is good to see you both still do that,' says Nabi.

'What, this? Otherwise how would children keep arriving in this house?'

'Hush, woman.'

'Your brother isn't a child. He has seen things you never will.'

'Those nice German girls? Perhaps I will see them too.'

'Much good it will do you, old man.' His sister-in-law reaches up behind her to fondle her husband's beard. 'You have your brother's eyes, Nabi. And no beard to hide your face behind. Has no girl there noticed?'

Nabi shrugs.

'There must be Afghan girls. There are no nieces or daughters or younger sisters at the mosque? In your circle of friends?'

'Why must he look for an import when the local pool is full?'

'You keep quiet. Nabi, you are careful, aren't you? At the hospital?'

'I wear a mask. I wear gloves. I obey all the rules. I don't want to be sick.'

'It pains me to think that you're caring for strangers at a time like this.'

'They aren't strangers to him.'

'They aren't his people.'

'If he meets a woman there and has a child, what will that child be? Will they be his people then? Our people?'

'You're just arguing for the sake of it.'

'Whether they're my people or not is irrelevant,' says Nabi pacifically. 'They are god's people. To care for them is the right thing to do.'

'Trust you to say that,' says his sister-in-law irritably. 'No, of course you're right. Don't mind me. I just worry about you. Even though I am proud of the work you do.'

'You know that, don't you?' says his brother. 'We are proud of you.'

'I know, brother. How is my nephew?'

His sister-in-law purses her lips. His brother looks down at her hair.

'He is still coughing. Still has a fever.'

'It is just a cold. Like every other one he has already had. It has to be. We know this in our minds.'

'It has to be. Who would have brought the sickness up here, at this time of year? Nobody has come from the outside since winter began.'

'Still, Nabi; after what you've told us, what we see on the news …'

'What you know in your mind doesn't affect what you carry in your heart.'

'He didn't sleep last night. Neither did we.'

Nabi looks at them disconsolately. He steels himself to the task.

'This is what you have to do,' he says finally. 'One of you has to choose to be with him. The other one has to stay away. You could both already have it, but we have to assume you don't. Do you understand?'

'What are you saying, Nabi?'

'I'm saying that you have other children. One of you has to be well to look after them. So, you have to choose. Who will be with him? It can't be both of you. Till he is better, and a few days after; only one of you can have any contact with him. The other has to stay away.'

His brother's stricken face fills the screen. 'How do we choose?'

'You are his parents, brother. It is your responsibility.' Nabi sighs. 'Look, all the indications are that young children aren't too badly affected. If he has it, he will recover quickly. Like all children do. I'm more worried about you two.'

His sister-in-law turns the phone to herself. 'Don't worry, Nabi. We will do as you say. I will make sure of it.' She touches her fingers to the screen, to his face. 'Be careful, please?'

'Do you remember what it was like before?'

'It was only a few weeks ago. Of course I do.'

'You know what I mean.'

'I know.' He too has felt the sensation of time simultaneously compressed and telescoping endlessly. There are hours when he feels nothing has changed, yet when he looks back, he has done things it would have taken him days to achieve in the time before the sickness.

His house has never been cleaner. His responses to his friends have never been quicker. Yet he feels no fulfilment.

'I would never check on my friends on Instagram. My real friends. You know? Because I was with them. I knew what they were doing and feeling and seeing. I didn't have to watch the playback as well.'

Nabi nods.

'Now ... I'm always on my phone. Watching them. Keeping tabs. But they're all stuck where they are, like me. What could they possibly be doing that would be of any interest to anyone else?'

But she can't look away, thinks Nabi. This is what human contact has come to. He wants to ask her whether she has posted about him on her feeds. Did her friends know she met an Afghan immigrant in the forest above her parents' home? Did she say he was nice, made the best tea, had a warm smile?

He has told nobody about her. What is there to tell? That he met a young German woman who walked her dog in the forest, and they sat and drank tea together from two ends of a wooden bench?

She puts her phone between them.

'Look.'

Nabi leans over, carefully avoiding touching her phone. Through the glare of the sunlight he sees a good-looking young man with his arm around a woman. They are smiling; they are clearly happy; her arms are around his waist.

It is her.

'Your boyfriend?'

'A friend. Who isn't here.'

Her finger flicks at the screen. That distant man cooks, tends plants on a little balcony, cuddles a teddy bear on a bed. The bed, his posture suggests, is big enough for two.

'He looks nice.'

She says nothing, flicking through the feed.

'Are you an active user yourself, or just a stalker?'

'Do you want to add me, Nabi?'

The question hangs in the air.

They look at each other from their respective ends of the bench, her phone between them like a challenge.

What would she see on my feed, thinks Nabi. An empty house? Simple dinners by myself?

My single bed?

Which is the better strategy for the single person on social media? Do we show each other the fullness of our lives, so others may marvel at them? Or do we tempt in the similarly lonely with the promise of spaces they may then fill in?

'Do you want my phone number?' she asks quietly. There is no mockery in her voice. 'I would like you to call me when you are lonely, Nabi. And I will call you when I am. Not just here. Not just over tea.'

'What is your number?' he asks finally.

He enters the digits she recites on his phone. From across the path comes the sound of children laughing. The young patient mother comes out of the still-bare trees, one child in her arms, the other running beside her. He sees Nabi and flies to his side. Nabi is already on the ground, laughing as the boy clambers on him. He attempts to keep the child away, but he pays him no heed and they are united in their delight in each other.

'Hallo,' says the mother with a smile. She stops as Nacho sniffs at her legs.

'Your children are so cute,' says the girl.

'Thank you.'

Now that she is close, now that they can hear her, it is clear that the young mother is a foreigner as well.

'Where are you from,' asks Mia politely.

'Bosnia.'

The girl nods.

'It is lovely up here, isn't it?'

'So nice.'

Her son, tiring of Nabi, bolts down the path. The woman trots off after him with a parting smile, her other child laughing in her arms.

Mia watches Nabi get up, dust himself off, park himself again on his end of the bench. 'You know them well?'

'Children don't wait to be formally introduced.'

She smiles. 'One month ago, you couldn't have paid me to have her life.'

'And now?'

'At least she has a reason to get out of bed in the morning.'

'Two,' says Nabi.

Mia shakes her head. 'She is beautiful, isn't she?'

'She is an angel.'

Mia nods. It is true. 'Will you call me, Nabi?'

'I will.'

'Good. Till then.' She walks away.

She calls him at night.

'What are you doing, Nabi?'

'I just ate, and now I'm cleaning up.'

'What did you eat?'

He looks at the debris of his meal. Chicken cooked with yoghurt, fried eggplants, fresh rotis from the Indian restaurant in the village, picked up at the back door, because the chef is a friend. The recitation surprises him. He hasn't even noticed the work he put in, thinking as he was of the treat to come.

'How wonderful,' she sighs. 'I just ate a sandwich for the eleventh straight meal. I think my mother is now officially out of sausage.'

'Pork?'

'What else? Oh, you don't eat it.'

'No, but I've often wondered what it tastes like.'

'Salty. Piggy.'

'That doesn't sound nice at all.'

'No, it really doesn't, when I put it like that.' She laughs. Nabi imagines her lying in her bed in her parents' home, her phone held up to her ear, her other hand perhaps playing with her hair.

'How is Nacho?'

'Snoring away in his basket.'

'He snores?'

'Like a jet engine. He's impossible.'

Nabi sits down by the window, so he can look out at the sea. How wide is her experience? How many snorers has she known?

'Did you speak to your brother today?'

'Earlier tonight.'

'What's happening with him?'

'They are well. Well, their younger son ... He hasn't been well. He has a cough. He can't sleep at night because he is having difficulty breathing. A fever. Headaches and chills.'

'Oh god.'

'No, I don't think it is the sickness. I mean, it isn't as if anyone goes up to our town at this time of year. My brother went through every arrival in the last three weeks. Nobody from outside has had any contact with them.'

'Umm.'

'Yes. That's how they feel. How I feel.'

'Is he getting better?'

'If he struggles again tonight ... they'll have to take him to Kabul.'

'You will know in the morning?'

'I will call as soon as I wake up.'

'I am sorry, Nabi.'

'Don't be. It isn't your fault.'

'No. But I wish I could help.'

'You are helping by speaking to me.'

'Well, if you can, imagine that I am there, there is no sickness, and I'm giving you the biggest hug.'

Nabi closes his eyes, even though the lake is its usual perfectly respectable self. He breathes in deeply, slowly exhaling so as not to give himself away.

If I were to meet someone here, he thinks; if I were to put down roots. If I were to have a family in this new world—

What wouldn't that change? Would anything remain the same?

'Nabi? Did I say something wrong?'

'No! I was just imagining you giving me a hug.'

He can't see her, but he thinks he feels her smile.

'Well, don't get carried away,' she says briskly. 'That one is meant to be shared between your nephew and yourself.'

'Till tomorrow, then.'

'Till tomorrow. Don't be late. Nacho doesn't like it.'

His nephew didn't need the trip to Kabul. He recovered quickly, as children do.

He is gratified to see how glad she seems when he tells her, the next morning.

This is the rhythm of their days. The tea and their courteous wandering conversations in the sun while Nacho dozes at their feet. The more daring exchanges at night, as he strolls about his small apartment, as she lies in her childhood bed.

What does she smell like when she is at home? What does she wear? Does she shed her mask entirely?

Nabi longs to stand behind a woman and brush out her hair. To be domestic with someone, to know them completely, to be without artifice. In the end, to be naked.

He told a friend once of his wish. That man had laughed and called him a poet.

'I'll be happy with a woman's breasts, Nabi. I don't need her hair as well.'

'You can't want both?'

'That's just greedy.'

Greed isn't always bad.

When it ended, Nabi was just sad that he hadn't been more greedy in the short time he had.

Was it even a week, he thought to himself, as he looked out at the silver See. A week of me sitting by this window and her lying in bed, talking comfortably, quietly, secretly to each other.

Did she ever touch herself as she spoke to me?

Their solitudes had always been of a different order. Her loneliness was only as old as the sickness, while he had been alone since he left his home.

Their last day together—

'It has been a week since my nephew got better.'

'I know. How is he?'

'Completely recovered. Have you heard from your parents?'

'I did. Their tickets have been changed. The airline will honour them when they can fly.'

'When is that?'

'Perhaps as early as two weeks.'

Nabi nods.

'You were right, Nabi. Things are improving.'

Over the past week, Nabi has seen fewer and fewer cases of the sickness coming in to the hospital. He doesn't want to jump the gun, he tells her; he doesn't want to jinx it, but it seems that the worst is over.

He is on the frontline. His information is valid and current. Even his co-workers are in a better mood.

Across the way they hear the happy laughter of the Bosnian woman and her children. Nacho ambles over to say hello as they come out of the forest. Nabi watches the boys frolicking around the old dog as their mother looks on, smiling.

'Paradise.'

'One version of it.'

'It doesn't appeal to you anymore?'

'Now that I actually may have options again? I don't know. I have to think about it.'

Nabi nods. 'Will you go back to Berlin? Once all this is over?'

'I won't go till I know what is happening with my family. I can't leave Nacho alone.' She looks at him. 'I won't just leave, Nabi. You know that, right?'

He smiles, squinting into the warming sun. The memory of the night before is a blanket over both of them. He stretches, relaxes more deeply into its embrace.

'Besides, Berlin ...' says Mia meditatively. 'Everyone is talking about how this sickness is an opportunity to rethink things, to start again.'

Nabi listens quietly.

'My life there ... That man ... There are other things in this world. Aren't there?'

Nabi looks at the family and Nacho at play. The older boy is kneeling on the ground, his arms tightly around the old dog. Nacho's eyes are closed against the sun. He rubs his head against the little boy's face.

A man can dream, thinks Nabi.

He feels her lightly touch his arm with the tip of one finger. He looks at her enquiringly.

'More tea?' she asks.

He holds out his cup.

She doesn't answer her phone at night. The first, or the second time he calls.

He tells himself she is busy. He cooks his solitary meal, sits by his window, does what he has done a thousand times before. He goes out on his little balcony and records the Croatian next door singing as he cooks for his family. He goes for a walk by the lake. He circles it six times before he goes back inside.

He tries her again, then once more, an hour later.

The moon is bright that night. It keeps him awake, no matter where he puts his pillow.

The Bosnian woman passes him in the morning.

'Beautiful day.'

'The best!'

The elder boy clambers up on the bench next to Nabi, the younger one toddling at his feet. Nabi smiles as they play around him.

'You heard the news?'

'Of course.'

'When might their father be expected to ... return?'

'Perhaps today.'

'That soon?'

They look at each other quietly. The government has decided the worst is over. A semblance of normal life is set to resume.

She smiles, then. What else is there to do? She has been polite enough to ignore that he is sitting by himself for the first time in weeks. Now it is her sons who people his bench.

Sometimes it is her smile he sees as he drifts off to sleep, the way she looks at her children, the quiet courage that folds the fatigue around her eyes and mouth into the creases that illuminate the world for those around her.

She really is an angel. Any man should have counted himself lucky to have had her in his life, to gird what is fragile and make it brim with love.

Any normal man.

She walks into the forest with her little family. The mother walks till she finds a place to sit, then they are hidden from him. Yet, he hears the happy cries of her children. The forest has been reborn, and they can play hide-and-seek in it again.

Nabi leans back against the bench, cracks his shoulders, bends his head this way and that.

He wishes he had brought some fruit up to eat in the sunlight, but he has fallen out of the habit these past few weeks. At least the sun isn't going anywhere.

From down the hill comes the sound of a siren on its way up to the Krankenhaus. Nabi picks up his still-full thermos of tea and turns back to where he works.

6

THE ANGEL

Nejla

Spring 2020

The girl walks out of the forest alone.

It is barely 7 a.m. The first dogs haven't yet completed their morning rounds, their humans trudging behind. The sun is still hidden behind the hill.

Uli should still be in bed. Awake for hours, but resolutely under the sheets. What is there for him to do outside?

His bladder drives him out of what should be his refuge. And then, well, what is the point of getting back under the covers?

He brews himself a pot of coffee, picks up the newspaper from the mailbox, settles down on the balcony with a blanket around his shoulders. Liesl is still asleep.

She sleeps as she always has. Soundlessly, her hands crossed over her heart like a corpse arranged for viewing.

When they were first married, he would lean over to check her breathing, to see if she were still alive. As he grew more used to her silence, he would treasure these minutes when he had her to himself. When even she wasn't there. Just him, her sleeping form, the steady rise and fall of her breast. He would hold her and close his eyes again as their room lightened.

Now, he envies her repose.

He is deep in a story buried in an inside page when he notices the girl.

She is dressed oddly. As if for a party, and not the forest. She isn't wearing a dress or heels, but neither is she equipped for the morning chill this early in the year. She hurries, he feels, because she is cold. Her thin jacket is worn over a t-shirt below. Her arms are tight across her chest.

She looks up at him as she passes. He notes her smudged eyes. There seem to be twigs caught in her hair.

She appears wan, hungover.

His eyes follow her as she disappears down the street, bound for the village.

Liesl comes out later in a dressing gown. She bends down to kiss his head, pours herself a cup of coffee. She pulls on a blanket of her own.

'Look at this,' he says.

She says nothing. He will speak into the void, she knows.

'Indonesia. Ramadan has started.'

She nods. His habit of starting stories without explanatory notes is familiar as well.

'They go back to their villages.'

This is the way of the world.

'Except, this year, they can't. Because of the illness.'

'A law?'

'The villagers themselves. Outsiders aren't welcome.'

'But the people going home aren't outsiders.'

'No, they aren't.'

'That seems unfair.'

He grunts. The story doesn't need to have a moral payoff to be of interest. 'The world,' he says, with a shake of his head. 'Such things.'

Liesl sips her coffee and closes her eyes.

'I saw the strangest thing,' he says with a start. 'A girl down there, not one hour ago. But she was dressed for a night out. Who does that to go walking in the forest?'

Liesl shrugs. Nobody that she can think of.

'She looked drunk. You know, like they do when they've been out.'

Liesl says nothing. Her interest is already fading.

'Do you think these kids are having parties up there? All night?'

'In our forest?'

'With the sickness! It would be completely mad!'

'Did you recognise her?'

'No. But there are so many strangers these days.'

'She's probably on a train home by now.'

'In the forest! Idiots.'

'Perhaps it is the only place they have.'

'Liesl, they shouldn't be meeting at all.'

She just looks at him. He shakes his head again and goes back to his newspaper.

'Mia told me she spoke with you?'

'Oh yes. I saw she's back. We should have her over.'

Liesl nods. 'I'm walking with her today. I'll ask her.'

'Ask her about that girl, will you? If young people are meeting up there?'

'Oh god.'

'It is against the law. It is unsafe for people to meet in groups right now.'

That much is indisputably true.

'We don't know who these people are,' says Uli plaintively.

She sighs. 'I'll ask her.'

'That young man.'

Mia looks at the old woman sideways.

'Oh come, Mia. You know.'

The younger woman giggles. 'Nabi.'

'Yes. Him.'

'What about him?'

'You know him?'

'Clearly.'

'You meet him every day. With your dog.'

'The forest has eyes!'

'Yes, it does. Is he a nice man?'

'He's a very nice man.'

'He is good to you?'

'He makes me tea.'

'That's all?'

'It really is.'

Liesl looks keenly at the young woman, who looks back guilelessly. Liesl smiles and shakes her head. 'You have never taken me seriously.'

'I'm a big girl, Tante. I'll be fine.'

'I'm sure you will. As you say, he's a nice man.'

They walk companionably under the trees, Nacho ambling slowly at their heels.

'Your uncle saw something odd this morning.'

Mia looks curiously at her.

'A young woman. Around your age, he said. Perhaps younger. Coming out of the forest.'

'What time?'

'Early. He couldn't sleep, so he was out on the balcony.'

Mia doesn't seem surprised.

'Are young people meeting in the forest, Mia?'

'Where else can they be together?'

'That's what I said. But you know him. He worries.'

'I can't say I blame him.'

'You go up as well?'

'There is nobody in this town that I want to meet up here.'

The old woman nods slowly. 'How do they locate each other?'

'There are apps.'

'Aren't they worried they'll be found out?'

'At night? Up here? Who will find them?'

Liesl looks around herself. The three of them have the forest to themselves.

'This forest eats everything, Tante. Even noise. You know that.'

Liesl nods.

'For those few hours, while they're together, I suppose it eats their loneliness as well,' says the young woman quietly.

The old woman stops, her breathing suddenly heavy on the air. Mia puts a hand to her shoulder in concern.

'I'm fine, child. Don't worry. I just want to catch my breath.' She breathes deeply, slowly, finding a rhythm again. 'There *is* one person you want to meet up here. Isn't there?'

The two women smile.

'Nejla.'

'How do you spell that?'

The Bosnian spells it out.

Her sons play around them. They run between the sunlight and the shade, their steps skipping through the leaves. The older one leading, the younger one feeling his way, getting better every minute of every day. Ahilya could watch them forever, she feels. But adult interactions have their own gravity. She drags herself back to smile at the woman standing across from her.

'I have known Nejla for some time now,' says Liesl gently.

'Since I was carrying my little one.'

'You still carry him everywhere!'

'He likes it so.'

'So do you. Don't you?'

Nejla acknowledges the truth of it with a small, shy smile. Her face is open; it is clear; her pleasure is genuine.

She has no malice, feels Ahilya with sudden clarity. She is complete. She has her children and she wants nothing else.

The thought infuriates her. So she forces herself to smile. Again.

'They grow up so quickly. Before I know it, he'll be gone.'

'To another woman's arms,' murmurs Liesl.

Nejla's smile widens. It is a distant prospect, that these beautiful creatures will one day be men with lives and loves of their own. That glimpse of a future yet undefined makes her glow.

How lucky her children are, thinks Ahilya. To see that face every day.

'Things are getting better, now,' says Liesl.

'The sickness, you mean?'

The old woman nods.

A shadow crosses Nejla's face. She shakes it off quickly. 'It is good to know that things will be back to normal soon.'

'We don't know that will happen,' says Ahilya shortly.

'We don't know if it will last. There is a difference,' says Liesl.

'A small one.' Ahilya, sharply.

'An important one.' Liesl, equably. 'At least to me. I am too old to think too far into the future. I'm more worried about tomorrow.'

'You aren't that old. You have to see my sons grow up!'

'Both of them? That may be too much to ask!'

Ahilya looks away to the children, playing now with her dog. They bend to her, put their faces to hers. She enjoys the attention, nips at their hands gently. They shriek with delight. They run, she gives chase. It is all as it should be.

'Your sons ...' Ahilya stops. She hasn't the words.

'I know. I mean, I'm their mother. But I know.'

Her face is turned to her children. She literally bristles with happiness.

What must it be like, thinks Ahilya, to feel like that. Did I ever feel like that?

She wants to sink to her knees by this woman's side, to put her face against her, to hug her close. To know her as her children do.

Nejla steps after her sons. Ahilya whistles to her dog. Liesl looks at her in enquiry.

'Shall we?' says Ahilya.

'Did you not like her?'

'I think I like her too much.'

'That worries you?'

'She is nothing like me.'

Liesl nods. 'Speak to her. Without me.'

'I'm sorry?'

'I can manage the walk home by myself.'

Ahilya watches the old woman slowly walk away.

Theirs is not an easy friendship, at least not to begin with.

Their conversation is stilted. Nejla's English is serviceable, while Ahilya's German has improved exponentially since she met Liesl. But common ground is hard to find.

'How long have you been here?'

'Six years, now.'

'Were both your sons born here?'

'They are German.'

Questions with short answers, while good for forms in immigration offices, aren't as useful elsewhere. They sit, one to each end of a tree trunk, watching the boys play with the dog.

Ahilya wants to ask the other woman how she lives. She has no visible means of support, yet her children don't look hungry. Does she work?

If she does, it is clearly for a very understanding employer. One that allows her limitless time off during the workday to play in the forest with her children.

If she doesn't work, how does she manage?

It is the sort of question a woman like her would have asked without any qualms in her past life. Beyond Indians using queries like these as conversation starters; professionally, she would have needed all the facts before she dispensed advice to the women in need before her. If you cannot ask, how can you help?

But this world is different, she is still a stranger to this country, she doesn't know its rules. The woman at the other end of the fallen tree is her equal. She isn't standing before her as a supplicant.

She cannot question blithely anymore. It is another loss she must reckon with.

The Bosnian senses the Indian woman's hesitation. She smiles at her.

'It is not easy to be new in a place.'

'No. It really isn't.'

'The illness makes it worse, yes?'

Ahilya can only nod.

'Liesl is a good friend. I am glad you found her.'

'I think she found me.'

The other woman smiles, again. 'Shall I tell you about Bosnia,' she says lightly. She starts to speak in English without waiting for a reply.

She speaks of the seasons, her home in the old place, her father who is sick and her mother who will live forever, and how they sit and smoke every evening as they watch the news. There are uncles, cousins, pets in homes she hasn't entered in years; meals and feasts and choice dishes she wishes she could eat in this foreign place. There are friends; there is warmth; echoes and whispers of a world she still inhabits in her heart and mind, a place that warms her when it is cold where she is.

Her voice is gentle as she feels her way through the unfamiliar words. The effect is lulling, and Ahilya feels her eyes growing heavy.

It is a moment before she realises the other woman has stopped and is looking at her.

'I feel as if I was there,' says Ahilya. It sounds lame even to her own ears.

There is a small smile at the corner of the Bosnian's mouth. 'We sleep a lot there as well.'

Ahilya feels herself blushing, but the smile on the other woman's face is disarming and real and so her own face relaxes and then she laughs.

'Thank you for letting me talk so much,' says Nejla sincerely. 'I wouldn't normally be so rude.'

'You're not rude at all!'

She really isn't. She just wants to speak. Even with her children, thinks Ahilya. Even within that little circle of light, she is alone. Just as I am.

'I haven't spoken that much in months.'

No, thinks Ahilya. None of us have. 'Shall I tell you about India?'

'I would like that. I have always wanted to go.'

The words trickle out of the Indian. Soon it is a stream, and then a flood, washing over the song of the blackbirds and the finches. The children come and get a snack, the dog is given water, the light moves imperceptibly from directly overhead toward the edge of the clearing.

'Thank you for listening,' says one of them eventually. They are walking out of the forest, now, the children and the dog with them.

The blackbirds are in full voice around them.

'Do they speak with each other, or at each other?'

'The birds? Are they in conversation, you mean?'

'Umm.'

'Why do you care? Their noise is a gift.'

'Beggars can't be choosers?'

'Contact is a blessing. Accept it.'

'She is nothing like me.'

'Why is that a bad thing?'

'She is nothing like you, is she?'

No. She really isn't.

'She isn't like me either. Is she, bhainji?'

No.

'I came to you, bhainji. I sought you out,' continues Harpreet, gently.

Ahilya listens.

'Our relationship is ... different. I know that. It could only happen here. In this way. I am comfortable with that.'

'You helped me too, Harpreet. You know this. In a way nobody else could.'

Harpreet acknowledges it, bending her head gracefully. 'This woman ...'

'Nejla.'

'Lovely name.'

'Isn't it?'

'She is educated. She is young. She could be anything.' Yet her life is her children. 'This bothers you.'

Of course it does. How could it not?

'Does she need your help?'

'She hasn't asked.'

'Will she?'

Ahilya is quiet.

'If she does ask, what will you say?'

'Liesl.'

There is no answer.

'*Liesl.*'

Uli walks out to the balcony, but she isn't there either. Is she already in the forest with her friend?

Well, I have friends too, he thinks. The sun is up. I'll go see what Gerd is doing.

He walks slowly down the street, past the quiet houses, the well-tended gardens. A man walking in the other direction steps into the street to give him right of way. Uli nods briefly. He doesn't know the other man, but he appreciates the gesture. He fumbles in his pocket. Has he forgotten his mask?

Bother it, he thinks irritably. We'll be sitting outside anyway. If someone wants to report me, they're more than welcome.

He rings the bell. The woman he has known for most of his life answers the door, her questioning face relaxing into a smile of welcome. She bustles back into the house, shouting for her husband. She pops her head out of the door, tells Uli to walk around to the back. There's a table set up under the tree in their garden. He should get settled while she rousts the man of the house out of his hole.

Uli picks his way through the shrubbery that threatens to overrun the flagstone path. In years past, the small weeds between the stones would have been painstakingly picked out. A slim hand-held tool; a cushion to kneel on; a tall glass of something nice at the end as an inducement. A weekend ritual repeated up and down this street, this town, this land.

Such are the hours we used to order our lives by. And now the minutes and the seconds slip away unheeded, and gardens slip their bounds out of sight of passers-by.

He mops at his brow under the hat he has worn against the sun.

Uli hears his name, the gruff voice of his almost-friend, a tray holding beers and a couple of glasses in his hands. They bump knuckles awkwardly, the greeting odd to them both.

'It is good to see you.'

They open, pour and drink. They exhale.

'How is Liesl?'

Uli shrugs.

'In her garden?'

'When she's not in the forest.'

'Really? I don't know if I could make it up there anymore.'

'She's kept herself in good health.'

'She really has.'

They sit among the playthings that await the return of Gerd's grandchildren. There is a trampoline and a little goal. There are myriad balls, a table set up with small chairs, a solitary tricycle in a corner. To one side, propped against the wooden fence, is a portable pool. It is packed away right now, but Uli knows it can fold out to something reasonably substantial. Something young children would look forward to when on their way to see their grandparents; to be used as an inducement when they're not in the mood to see the old people.

Did my daughter play with Gerd's sons in this garden, he thinks. Wasn't there a birthday party, once, and a pool like this one, and a dozen screaming kids?

This space has known such things.

'A bit much for two old people like us, isn't it,' says Gerd quietly.

'It really is.'

'I can't even look after it anymore. But we kept it because the kids like it so.'

'Of course.'

'This fucking disease.'

'I *know*.'

'I'm happy to see you, Uli. But can I ask you a favour?'

'Anything.'

'Let's not talk about being lonely. If I do, anymore, I may go mad.'

Uli sits back in his chair, raises his cool glass to his closed eyes.

Ignore it enough. And it might go away.

They sit quietly under the tree, the two old men, drinking their beer.

'Why did you come?'

'To this place? To work. What else?'

'Was it easy?'

'My company valued me, invested in me. I learnt a new language.'

'It was fun?'

'It was a challenge. Challenges can be stimulating. Once you're up to dealing with them.'

'Is that how you met your husband?'

'We met at a bar. We had a friend in common. He was sitting at the next table with a few friends. They joined us.'

'It was quick?'

'He was charming. Handsome. Interested.'

Ah. *Interested*. Such a rare thing. 'It *was* quick.'

'Very.'

They smile together. Even a nightmare can begin well.

'What are we, if we don't remember the way it is when it starts?'

'Love, you mean?'

The Bosnian nods gently. The Indian can only agree.

'You know about the way he treated me?' Nejla asks quietly.

'I do.'

'You wonder why I haven't gone back?'

'To Bosnia? Not at all.'

Nejla looks at her.

'This is your home. Your boys were born here. Why should a man chase you away?'

Nejla nods, again. 'This part of my life belongs here.'

'Do you wish it had been somewhere else?'

'With someone else?'

'Umm.'

Nejla shrugs. 'Wishing won't make it so.'

It really won't.

'The police do what they can. The agencies as well. The people here are very good. They make an effort.'

'Then why is he still a threat?'

Again, she shrugs. 'Sometimes I think I am partly to blame.'

'How is it your fault?'

Nejla laughs. It is sudden, clear, merry. 'Oh, I don't blame myself for the way that man treated me. I really don't.' She looks at the Indian woman squarely. 'I am not a victim. Not like that.'

'Then ...'

'That first time ... Even the second. I should have been stronger in what I wanted. But my sons were still his children. He was still my husband.' She shakes her head. 'I should have let that asshole go to jail.'

'Has he ever touched the boys?'

'Not once.' She is definite.

'Well, that's a blessing.'

'Why? Just because he hasn't yet doesn't mean he wouldn't. He did it to me.'

Ahilya feels dazed at the other woman's clarity. The children come running back into the clearing, Ahilya's little dog barking madly at their heels. They are flushed from the sport. Their faces glisten. The dog pants and flops at her feet. The kids give off the smell of children in spring, of heavy jackets worn just a day too long. They lose their coverings as they clamber over their mother, and she laughs and kisses and dispenses water and treats.

'Has their father ever hit them?'

'They haven't brought it up.'

'She says he never has.'

'Why would she lie?'

'Have they seen her suffer?'

'I haven't asked.'

'Would they tell you?'

'They are children. We don't talk of these things.'

'What do you talk about?'

She pants, her tongue lolls, she rolls over on her side. She closes her eyes.

Well? What do you talk about?

'Why aren't we friends?'

'Aren't we?'

'You know what I mean.'

The woman of the house comes out, brings bread, olives out of a bottle, some cheese. Another beer is offered, but at their age, alcohol can no longer be dispatched as it was when they were in their pomp. Every journey to a bathroom is fraught with obstacles.

It is enough to be outside, in the shade, while the sun warms the rest of the world.

'Sometimes I feel as if I never really had any friends.'

'Umm.'

'There was always something to do. To get. A degree. A job. A wife.'

'Kids. Cars.'

'A house.'

'Yes.'

'All this talk of connection.'

'I connected with their mother, didn't I?'

'Our children had time for friends. They went abroad together when they were young. They travel together with their families now.'

'We didn't do any of that.'

'Who had the money?'

'Who had the time?'

Neither of them, they both agree. Now, they are meditative.

'Was it all worth it?'

'Those years?'

'The work. The discipline. The pushing.'

'All that effort.'

'Always, the effort.'

'It made this possible. All of this.'

'Then something like this comes along ...'

'We are alone.'

'Exactly.'

We were always alone.

'If something were to happen to her ...'

'If my Liesl were to slip, up there in the forest ...'

Two old men, waiting for the axe to fall, the motor to stop, the production line to finally be switched off. Both of them; all of them: blundering in the dark towards the knacking yard.

'You promised me, Uli.'

'We shouldn't speak of these things.'

No. We really shouldn't.

'I don't want us to be two sad old men. Come on, eat something.'

They eat, quietly.

'Why don't you come up to mine, tomorrow? Have a coffee with me? I'll put a table out for us in the garden.'

Gerd grunts. His wife wanders out. She has heard the last exchange.

'Go up there. What are you doing here?'

'Leave me alone, please.'

'No, you leave me alone. I would like some time to myself. You go up there tomorrow.'

Her husband rolls his eyes. Uli laughs.

'Put the table out, Uli. I'll make sure he comes.'

Later, at home—

Liesl and the Indian woman are puttering around in the garage. Uli watches them from the balcony.

'What are you looking for,' he asks finally.

'That electric saw you use on the small trees.'

'The rechargeable one? Why?'

'She needs it for her garden. There's no electric outlet there.'

Uli glances at the other woman. She is looking evenly at him. He turns away.

'On the shelf. Above the lawnmowers.'

'Ah, yes.'

'She'll need protective glasses if she's using that. It is powerful. There are some right there. Next to the charger cord.'

'Where?'

'*There*, Liesl. And gloves.' He looks at Ahilya. 'Have you gloves?'

She shakes her head silently.

'Take mine,' he says. The woman nods her thanks. He acknowledges it briefly, before retreating into his home.

'It comes suddenly, doesn't it?'

'Love?'

'Yes.'

'Were you happy? In the beginning?'

'Very.'

'Me too.'

Today, it rains. The boys wear jackets and gumboots. Liesl stands under her umbrella while they sport around her. The still, grandmotherly figure in the centre of the clearing, rain sloping off her umbrella; the young boys stomping through the puddles around her, water jumping back off the earth towards the rain; the dog, sodden, yapping, demanding to be included: it is an image Ahilya feels she has seen before. It is like something from the sort of movie she has avoided her whole life.

To be manipulated by the blandly adorable is to be wilfully ignorant. But things have changed.

She is no longer a passive auditor of the boys' lives. Their beauty is a pain in her side. She feels their yells. She turns her head when they are out of sight and out of hearing, yearning to see where they are, mindful of danger.

She feels invested. In Liesl as well.

The Bosnian is part of that circle.

'Did it go just as quickly?'

'It wasn't a switch, no. Not even the first time he hit me. It was such a shock. To both of us, I think. I couldn't believe it had happened.'

'And then?'

'It happened again. And again. And then I wasn't in love with him anymore.'

'No lingering feelings?'

'None.' It is flat. Final. Believable.

'Good.'

'Yes. That would complicate things.'

Nejla smiles at the scene in front of her. 'I don't know what I would have done without her.'

'Liesl?'

The Bosnian nods.

'She's something, isn't she?'

'She really is.'

'So much patience.'

'You have no idea.'

Ahilya looks at the other woman, surprised at her sudden vehemence. Nejla considers her in turn, the now-familiar small smile lurking.

'What?' asks Ahilya.

'Can you keep a secret?'

'Depends what it is.'

'I can't tell you if I don't know your answer.'

'That is a problem, isn't it?'

They look at each other quietly.

This is important, Ahilya knows. It is a crossroads, and she must choose wisely. She closes her eyes against the weight. She feels the wet fur of her dog against her leg.

'I am sorry, Ahilya. I shouldn't have asked.'

'No, you absolutely must ask.'

'Ok. Let me put it another way. Will you help me? Help my sons?'

'Anything.' Of this she is sure. 'All you have to do is ask.'

'Anything?'

'Should I have said no?'

'Not at all. I think you're doing the right thing.'

'We must help each other.'

'Well, we must help her in this case. Because she needs it.'

'What does she need?'

'Do you really not know?'

She opens her eyes. Liesl is standing next to Nejla. They look at her quietly.

'Anything,' she repeats.

It is nice, feels Uli, to be sitting in the garden with someone other than his wife. His friend made the big trip up the street, his body bent, grumbling against the slope. He sits on the other side of the table, eating the cake Uli found in a tin, drinking the coffee that is freshly brewed. Gerd sighs in contentment, leaning back against the seat, brushing a crumb of cake off his chest.

'Not so bad, is it?'

'Not at all.'

'Nice little garden, this. All Liesl's work, right?'

'When she needs something lifted, or cut down, she does ask.'

'Yes, but that's normal. I wish my wife took more interest. Instead of making that bloody house sparkle. Who is coming over?'

'At least your house is clean.'

Gerd grunts. It is clearly not something he values currently. 'Where is she?'

'Liesl? In the forest. She's always up there.'

'Oh yes. You said so.'

Uli grunts as well, helping himself to more cake.

'Who does she go with? Not by herself, surely?'

'This Indian woman.'

'A foreigner? Why?'

Uli bends his head towards the road. Sure enough, coming down from the forest, on the other side of the hedge, are Liesl and the Indian. They laugh as they walk, carrying something between them. A large shopping bag, a handle each in their hands.

Uli claps his hands.

'Liesl!'

The women stop, looking at the hedge.

'In the garden! Gerd's here.'

Liesl peers through the hedge, smiling as she sees the visitor.

'Hallo, Gerd. I didn't know you were coming.'

'I hope it is no trouble?'

'None at all, as long as my man takes good care of you.'

'You won't join us?'

'No, we're headed to my friend's house.'

'What's in the bag?'

'Stones and things. For her summer garden.'

'Is it heavy? Shall I help?'

'Just eat your cake. I'd hate to have to explain a slipped disc to your wife.'

There is a snort of laughter. The Indian woman waits patiently for the conversation to end, a small smile on her lips for the unseen people on the other side of the hedge.

Liesl says her goodbyes, and the women leave, their shopping bag hefted between them.

'Nice woman, that?'

'I haven't said two words to her.'

'She seemed alright.'

'Liesl likes her.'

'That's what matters, isn't it?'

Uli nods. That truly is all that really matters.

'Hallo, Tante!'

'Hallo, darling. Where are you off to?'

'Nacho wanted a walk. We're off to the forest.'

'Are you sure he can manage the trip up there?'

Mia looks at Liesl, an eyebrow raised. The penny drops and the old woman smiles in her turn. 'Will that nice young man be up there?'

'If he isn't, I'll be upset. I've got my tea mug.'

'Is that your ritual?'

'What else can we do, right now?' She stops, as if struck by something. She claps a theatrical hand to her mouth. 'What if he tries to kiss me?'

'You're a big girl, darling. You'll know what to do.'

The woman at Liesl's side has been listening quietly. Mia stops and turns to her.

'I've seen you up in the forest. Nabi knows you, doesn't he?'

'My name is Ahilya.'

'I'm Mia.'

'Pleased to meet you.'

'And you. Our dogs seem to know each other already.'

'They do, don't they?'

'What's in the bag, Tante? I've seen you this whole week, carrying things back from the forest.'

'Just some things for Ahilya's garden.'

'Need help?'

'Isn't there a young man waiting for you?'

Mia smiles and pulls Nacho away from the bag he is sniffing at. The two women wave and turn back towards the Indian's home, their load shared equally between them.

They walk, this time, towards the hospital.

Liesl lags behind with the boys. The dog trots by their side. Nejla and Ahilya walk at her pace, stopping when she does, picking it up when she quickens.

'It is nice, once you get used to it,' murmurs Nejla.

'Being on doggie time? Well, unless you have something else to do. Then it's a pain.'

'I have nowhere else to be.'

Ahilya sighs. It is true for her as well.

The sun peeks out from behind the clouds. And immediately it is warmer.

Through the trees they see a man sitting on a bench. He is looking at a girl who is leaving. She leads a dog. She waves at the man, who waves back. He turns his face to the sun as she walks away.

'Do you know him?' Ahilya is curious.

'Nabi? Who doesn't?'

Ahilya chuckles. 'How did you meet?'

'He said salaam to me one day. I know the word. I responded.'

'He is polite.'

'Charming. You know what I liked best about him?'

'What?'

'He practically ignored me.'

'He ignored *you*?'

Nejla laughs out loud at Ahilya's disbelief. 'He played and played with my sons. He made such a fuss over them. They reminded him of his own nephew back home.'

The sound of her sons running down the path behind them turns her around.

'He wasn't lying. Of that, I am sure.'

Ahilya says nothing.

'When they see him, they will run to him. You watch.'

'Are children such good judges of character?'

'Better than me. I mean, look at my husband.'

There is no arguing with that.

'A good man,' muses Ahilya, looking at the quiet man alone on his bench, his eyes closed and his face turned to the sun.

'Nabi helped me.'

'How?'

'Why don't you ask him?'

'Nabi.'

He smiles, invites her to sit at the end of the bench. If there were only one seat, she thinks, he would have gotten up and offered it to her. There is a courtliness to him that is appealing.

'You know her, she says?' They can see Nejla through the trees, walking towards her sons and Liesl.

He nods silently. He is, suddenly, guarded. He bends to the dog and chirrups in her ear.

'Nejla said you helped her. I am curious. What did you do?'

'It was nothing.'

'It must be something. She is full of praise.'

'Surprising?'

'No. You're clearly a good person. What did you do?'

He sighs. 'I was sitting here. It was a cold morning, but what can you do? A habit is a habit. I saw her coming up the hill. The trees were bare, you see. She was running. She was carrying the little boy, the other one was running with her. They were all crying. I knew her, but it didn't matter. Even if I hadn't, I would still have gone to her aid. You understand?'

'I do.'

'It is what people do.'

I'll have to take your word for it, thinks Ahilya. But she keeps quiet.

'I ran towards them. There was a man behind. He was screaming. I had my phone out. I called the police. He saw the phone in my hand and he stopped. I … I stood between them; you know, the man and her. I waited till he left. Till the police came.'

He needs a moment to collect himself.

'He was shouting the vilest things. About her. The boys.'

She sees that it was, *is*, hard for him. He can barely breathe. Even now.

'They're his children. How could he say that to them? How can a man be like that?'

Oh Nabi, she thinks. All the things you've seen. And you're still a boy scout. She knows, then, why so many people are drawn to this quiet man.

'Did the police come?'

'I told them what I saw. I told them I was available in case they wanted anything else. I mean, I heard him. I saw him. I saw his face. He was ready to kill someone.'

'What happened?'

'Nothing. I heard later that she asked for him to be released, provided he promised to go away. He's not allowed near them anyway. They could have put him in jail, but she … You'll have to ask her. It's her husband.'

'When was this?'

'Beginning of the lockdown. The first or second day.'

'What? Now?'

'Well, a few weeks ago.'

A glad cry breaks out, and then the boys are hurtling towards Nabi, who gets up before they can hug him. He smiles and holds them at arm's length, then kneels on the hard path so he can be the same level. He bumps knuckles with them in turn and then, before he knows it, one of them is on his back as he laughs and laughs and then he pulls them to him.

Their mother lets them play for a moment, then calls them off. It won't do to break the rules so brazenly. Not even with them as young as they are. Not even up here, in the forest.

The boys are reluctant to leave his side. A promise of more play is extracted, an assurance of baked treats made. They go up the path, hand in hand with their mother. Liesl, standing now on the edge of the path, watches quietly.

Nabi is still kneeling on the ground. 'I would do anything for those boys,' he says.

Ahilya knows he means it.

The mother is watching over her shoulder, as her boys pull her up the path.

She knows it too.

She wears the same small smile as she is pulled away.

'You never said he was here.'

'You never asked.'

'I thought, this entire time, that you were worrying about the end of the lockdown. That he would try and sneak back here then. When you said it was your fault ... Nabi told me that you asked the police to let him go.'

'That was my mistake. I am ready to be judged for it.'

'I don't judge you. You know that.'

'Of course you judge me. Even when you say you don't, you do.'

Ahilya shakes her head. This is a conversation she has had before, in her previous life. She isn't ready to have it again.

'Why didn't you tell me?'

Nejla shrugs.

Ahilya rubs her eyes. She feels tired. 'It doesn't really matter, I suppose. What did he say? When he left? Did he say when he would return?'

Nejla says nothing.

'Nejla?'

'Who says he left?'

Liesl, the Cuban, Ahilya, Nejla—

Four women. Not counting the dog.

They sit one to each corner of a table in the Cuban's bar. The children are on the floor, mumbling happily over a book and some cookies their host found in her kitchen. They are out of earshot.

'He came in the middle of the night,' says Nejla. Her voice is calm, as it always is. 'I heard something. I got out of bed and came to the door. It was open. I wanted him away from the boys, so I ran.'

'Where,' asks Ahilya.

'Up here. Into the forest.'

Ahilya knows now the explanatory notes are only for her. It is clear that the Cuban and the Bosnian know each other. Indeed, they've known each other for a while. They greeted each other with the ease of memories held in common.

She feels, the Indian woman, on shifting ground. The old woman looks on gravely, as she does. The others wait to be summoned back to the floor.

'Then?'

'It was quite bright. The moon was up. I had pulled on a pair of boots, a dressing gown. But it was fiercely cold. I could hear his footsteps crunching on the frost behind me.'

'Was he saying anything?'

'No. Just his breathing. The crunching. My own ... breath.

'I ran and ran. I have always been athletic. My wind was better than his. But he is a man. I was in a bathrobe, and he was angry. I was scared he would catch me.'

'What were you thinking?'

'I wasn't. Who does, when you run?'

'So ...'

'So. He slipped. He cursed. I knew he'd stopped. I knew then he wouldn't catch me. I turned back to him. He was lying there, holding his leg.'

'He couldn't move?'

'He would have moved. Eventually.'

Yes, he would have.

'He was so angry. His face ... He said he would kill us all.'

'You believed him?'

Three pairs of eyes look at her steadily.

'What did you do?'

'What do you think,' asks the Cuban laconically.

'There was a cairn to one side. I found a good rock.'

It is news to Ahilya that rocks can be classed in this way.

'I wish I could take it back, that I had called the police instead. But I can't. It is done.'

'Where is he?' asks Ahilya finally.

'In my freezer,' says the Cuban, lighting a cigarette. She exhales slowly. 'He can't stay there, you know. Once the lockdown is over, and I start having guests again; I'm going to need it.'

Ahilya looks at her.

'I'm probably breaking all sorts of rules already.'

Ahilya turns back to Nejla.

'The rock is in a stream. The earth where it happened has been turned over. There's been rain and snow since.'

'The body needs to be moved,' continues the Cuban. 'In pieces. Cut further, if necessary. Transferred to where it will be disposed of. There has to be a schedule. An efficient one.'

Well, naturally. This is Germany.

'His absence will be noticed once the lockdown is over,' says Liesl gently. 'People will make enquiries. Come up here, perhaps.'

Ahilya closes her eyes against the scene.

'My boys will be taken away from me,' says Nejla quietly.

'We can't have that,' says Ahilya at last.

'No,' agrees Liesl. 'We really can't.'

The introductions are made quickly, easily.

They sit on the deck of the Cuban's bar in the forest. The dog is at their feet. The host brings coffee out. It is a beautiful day, the overhanging trees dappling the light falling on them. Liesl and Ahilya had walked up first, while Harpreet joined, as planned, on her break.

She is glad, Harpreet tells Liesl, to finally make her acquaintance.

'I saw you earlier. With Ahilya.'

'You should have said hello.'

The younger woman shrugs. The sickness, says the gesture; the rule of two. Her natural diffidence. To approach a stranger at the best of times is never easy. Now ...

'It doesn't matter. We know each other now.'

The Cuban sits down with them. Ahilya bends to her dog after Harpreet is done petting her.

'She is ready.'

'How do you know?'

'Ask her.'

'What if she says no?'

'Who will she tell?'

They talk of what Harpreet does. Ahilya tells them of Harpreet's claim, that her furnaces can take care of anything.

'Anything,' repeats Liesl meditatively.

'Anything,' says Harpreet firmly. 'Provided it is small enough.'

'How small?'

'I'm sorry?'

'How small would it need to be?'

'What are we talking about?' Harpreet looks wonderingly at the other women around her. 'Do you need me to dispose of something?'

They look back gravely.

'Tell her.'

The silence gathers around them.

'Tell her.'

So they do.

She looks at Ahilya for guidance. The other woman doesn't look away.

Harpreet doesn't run.

'It is necessary?'

'We wouldn't ask otherwise.'

There is nobody else they can turn to. Only she can do what is required.

More coffee comes out. The shadows shift, and still they chat. She specifies a size and a schedule.

The other women listen, take notes, arrive at an understanding. The dog is at rest at their feet.

They meet, finally, in the forest.

They nod at each other. Harpreet steps forward. She raises a hand, puts it to Nejla's shoulder. The Bosnian's eyes crinkle at the touch.

'Thank you.'

'It is nothing,' says Harpreet in reply.

'It is the world to me. To my children.'

'I have seen them. They are worth it.'

'I wish you the same blessing in your life.'

'Children? They aren't for everyone.'

'True. But love is.'

'Which means?'

'I wish for you to know what it is to love someone so much you would do anything for them.' Nejla puts her own hand up, then, to cover Harpreet's. 'Though what you are doing, right now ... Perhaps you are already there. I don't know if I could have done it for you.'

'Yes, you would,' says Ahilya.

'Yes, you would,' agrees Harpreet.

The dog stands quietly to the side.

Today, she has nothing to add.

They stand together, the four of them. In silence, as the forest returns to bloom.

'What's wrong, darling?'

'I think I made a big mistake, Tante.'

'Tell me.'

'Nabi.'

'Did he do something?'

'He didn't *do* anything. We both did.'

Liesl listens, her face neutral.

'I know it was silly. I just ... I needed the contact.'

'Of course you did. Everybody does.'

'Yes, but now? I mean, how many rules have I broken? What if I'm sick? What if he is?'

'You should go away.'

'Where?'

'Your parents' cabin. Do they still have it?'

'Of course.'

'You have the key?'

'I know where it is.'

'Take the dog. Go.'

'Tante ...'

'You need time to think, darling. This will give it to you. Away from him.'

'Why must I go away?'

'Will you stay away from him if you're here?'

The young woman flushes. The older woman's position is understandable.

'Just a few days,' says Liesl quietly, authoritatively. 'No more, or people will start to worry.'

'A few days?'

'Do you need more?'

The young woman shakes her head uncertainly. Perhaps the time suggested is enough. She will only know when she goes away.

'Turn your phone off,' says Liesl.

'Is that important?'

'Can you be alone when you have it on?'

'If I have it, I'll use it.'

'Then leave it with me.'

'What would I do without you?'

'Don't worry, child. You, of all people, have done nothing wrong.'

The young woman smiles with gratitude. The old woman smiles back, her love for this girl she has known her entire life evident. 'I'll look after you, my Mia. No matter what.'

Mia feels the words wash over her.

'I look after all my girls.'

The young woman doesn't hug her old aunt. The times won't allow it. But she knows the truth of the old woman's words. It has always been so, and she is grateful.

'This lockdown is almost over, isn't it?'

'Things are almost back to normal.'

'I'll do what you say, Tante. I'll be over in half an hour to drop off my phone.'

He is fully as courtly as Ahilya thought he would be.

The sight of Liesl labouring up the path brings him rocketing to his feet. He insists both women sit. The bench cannot accommodate all three of them if they are to sit the required distance apart. He is happy to stand.

Liesl catches her breath, then extends her hands to the young man, who takes them after a moment.

'I have been meaning to thank you in person, Nabi. For all you have done.'

'You don't need to. You know that.'

'I may need something else.'

He lowers his eyes, to the old hands in both of his own.

'Nejla may need something else,' says Liesl gently.

He nods, his head still down.

'The lockdown will be over soon. Perhaps as soon as tomorrow.'

'Yes.'

'We can't have any scrutiny. We're almost done, but we need a few more days. Till everything is put away.'

He keeps his peace.

'If it were to be required … If there were to be a … diversion …'

'I will do nothing more that is illegal.'

'All we need is for you to be quiet.'

He looks up. 'Does this have to do with Mia?'

'No harm will come to her. She is like a daughter to me. You know this.'

'What will you do?'

'The police will only ask you about Mia. *If* it comes to that. You can tell them the truth about the two of you.'

He looks away. He seems abashed. The old woman is unconcerned. 'They will know it anyway. Just, tell them slowly. Discreetly. All we need is for this to be over.'

'Does Mia know?'

'Not yet. Later …'

He closes his eyes.

'Nabi?'

'I'll do it.'

'You have to be quiet about all of this.'

'No matter what?'

'No matter what. Until the diversion isn't required anymore.'

Nabi exhales deeply, completely.

'We thank you,' says Liesl. 'She ... They thank you.'

'Were you there, Nabi,' asks Ahilya suddenly.

He says nothing.

'She must have needed a hand to get the body up to the bar. Did she call you?'

His hands drop Liesl's. They clench and unclench. 'I would do anything for those boys.'

'Of course you would, Nabi. So would we all. Otherwise why are we here?'

Ahilya looks at the old woman, the calm steel in her words.

'Innocence must be protected,' insists Liesl.

'Am I to have nothing good in this life?' he whispers.

'All you have to do is wait, child. You are a good man.'

'To be good is its own reward?' Nabi has heard it before, and he is still unconvinced. As is Ahilya.

But Liesl is resolute. 'Your deeds will be remembered. Your isolation has to end. Eventually.'

The world will be reborn. A new world in which, though Liesl is careful not to say it, anything will be possible.

Anything at all.

The two men lumber up the street against the slope. The coffee and cake that has become a part of their days must be earned. So, they walk beforehand. Nobody will report two old men strolling together. What good would it do?

Today, they see Liesl and the Indian woman walking towards them. They carry their bag between them, as per usual. They stop to exchange pleasantries as they cross each other. Gerd smiles at the Indian woman, who smiles back.

'Last day of the lockdown.'

'Yes, it is.'

'Are your grandchildren coming over?' ask Liesl.

'Tomorrow morning.'

'I am glad, Gerd. I know it has been hard for you.'

He nods. He knows the sympathy is sincere.

'Have you seen Mia,' asks Uli.

'No. Why?'

'There was a policeman outside her house. He said he was looking for her.'

'Whatever for?'

'God knows. I told him she was probably in the forest. He said he'd take a look.'

'I don't see why,' mutters Gerd. 'Nothing ever happens here. Or up there.'

'Nothing at all,' agrees Uli.

'Still carrying things down from the forest,' asks Gerd. He indicates the bag the women have between them.

'This is probably the last trip. It is getting a bit warm.'

The two old men look in the bag, at the moss, the odd distinctive stone, the bits of decorative wood. Liesl reaches into it to show them something, but the two men brush it off, resume their walk. The women amble off in the opposite direction.

'Pretty girl, that.'

'The foreigner? If she made a bit of an effort.'

'Why would she, with things the way they are? She can't go anywhere. Or meet anyone.'

'I suppose you're right.'

They flop into their seats in Uli's garden, mopping at their brows. It is a warm day. Summer may not be at hand, but it is certainly around the corner. Liesl's garden is ablaze.

'Did anything ever happen here,' asks Gerd suddenly.

'What do you mean?'

'All those years, Uli. When we were working. Raising families. Did we miss anything?'

Uli sighs. Lately he feels as if he has missed everything; that the world, somewhere in its revolutions around the sun, forgot he was along for the ride.

'Drink your coffee,' he urges his old friend. 'Your wife will be needing you back to get things ready.'

It won't do to have a dirty house when your family comes visiting.

7

THE LIGHT

The Reporter

August 2020

It is an absolutely scorching day.

It is August in Europe. Of course it is hot. The reporter turns the air-conditioning on in his car when he drives. The schools are on vacation. There are lines of people waiting outside the public swimming pool.

The spring lockdown is a memory. There are murmurings of a second wave, that the sickness is bound to return. But in the warm light of day, during the cool sleeveless dusk, when you are surrounded, again, by people at their tables under the sky, it seems mad to even consider the possibility. It is summer in a place that is mostly cold. If you can't be free now, then what use are you?

The playgrounds are at capacity in the evenings, kids on the apparatuses, their parents lurking to the side. All of them mask-less, in close proximity to each other. Polishing the sickness, passing it along, preserving it for eternity.

Perhaps they are just storing up these moments for when the isolation returns.

The reporter carries a mask everywhere. He is taking no chances.

He clears out his mailbox and steps into his home, hanging up his keys, taking off his sunglasses, stepping into his slippers. His old dog stirs out of his bed and trots over to say hello, knowing the man who has walked in will bend to his side, scratch behind his ear, murmur a question as to how his day has been.

They were up in the forest earlier. It has become a ritual. The two of them had ambled slowly down the shaded paths, stopping whenever his old friend needed a break, sniffed something intriguing, felt he could go no further.

He saw that same woman, as he did every day. A hat against the sun even though it was early, her boundless patience for the children playing at her feet.

He hasn't said a word to her all these days as he walked quietly by. But he knows her worlds are of interest, if he could just tell the story. The people she has known, the things she has seen.

Her deeds.

She smiles at him. He has walked past often enough.

He wishes he could speak to her. But that wouldn't do at all.

Her smile as he passes will have to suffice.

He looks out to the small side street he lives on, the quiet park beyond, the rows of neat houses with their perfect gardens that back up on it.

In the evenings, when it is cooler, he walks past those homes with his old dog at his side.

Wondering at the light and the lives inside.

ACKNOWLEDGEMENTS

This is a book about isolation, written theoretically in isolation, during the rolling lockdowns of 2020-21. But that isn't true of anything, is it?

I was listening to music. I read Chinese books in translation with my book club, and listened to podcasts. I cooked and walked, biked and ran. All those things, I did alone. But each of them changed me, and they changed *Into the Forest*. I am grateful to all the things I read and listened to in that time.

Sonal Shah and Amanda J. Fiore read early drafts. They *listened* to it, and made it so much better.

Karthika V.K. has been with me since my authorial life began in 2000; she's edited every book I've written. Ajitha G.S. has been my friend, colleague and conscience since we first met in 2006. Saurabh Garge brought my words to visual life with his design for the cover. Landing at Context was like coming home. To the team there, Amrita and Aatreyee, the sales team and everyone else: I love the oasis you've created in Delhi. I hope I can show more writers the way there.

The McEnteers, the Stahls, Erika next door: all our neighbours who supplied company when they could, and waved from balconies and windows when they couldn't.

Our families and friends who visited us when they were finally able to. My father, who has been everywhere we've lived, and always with me.

Christine, for being there.

Jagat, for the light. Always, the light.

And Figo, for love.

Thank you. Thank you. Thank you.